DUST

Mr. And Mrs. Haldeman-Julius

1st WORLD
LIBRARY
Literary Society

Dust

Mr. And Mrs. Haldeman-Julius

© 1st World Library – Literary Society, 2006
PO Box 2211
Fairfield, IA 52556
www.1stworldlibrary.org
First Edition

LCCN: 2006905704

Softcover ISBN: 1-4218-2133-8
Hardcover ISBN: 1-4218-2033-1
eBook ISBN: 1-4218-2233-4

Purchase *"Dust"*
as a traditional bound book at:
www.1stWorldLibrary.org/purchase.asp?ISBN=1-4218-2133-8

1st World Library Literary Society is a nonprofit
organization dedicated to promoting literacy by:

- Creating a free internet library accessible from any
computer worldwide.
- Hosting writing competitions and offering book
publishing scholarships.

Dust
contributed by Tim, Ed & Rodney
in support of
1st World Library Literary Society

CONTENTS

I

THE DUST IS STIRRED

DUST was piled in thick, velvety folds on the weeds and grass of the open Kansas prairie; it lay, a thin veil on the scrawny black horses and the sharp-boned cow picketed near a covered wagon; it showered to the ground in little clouds as Mrs. Wade, a tall, spare woman, moved about a camp-fire, preparing supper in a sizzling skillet, huge iron kettle and blackened coffee-pot.

Her husband, pale and gaunt, the shadow of death in his weary face and the droop of his body, sat leaning against one of the wagon wheels trying to quiet a wailing, emaciated year-old baby while little tow-headed Nellie, a vigorous child of seven, frolicked undaunted by the August heat.

"Does beat all how she kin do it," thought Wade, listlessly.

"Ma," she shouted suddenly, in her shrill, strident treble, "I see Martin comin'."

The mother made no answer until the strapping, fourteen-year-old boy, tall and powerful for his age, had deposited his bucket of water at her side. As he drew the back of a tanned muscular hand across his dripping forehead she asked shortly:

"What kept you so long?"

"The creek's near dry. I had to follow it half a mile to find anything fit to drink. This ain't no time of year to start farmin'," he added, glum and sullen.

"I s'pose you know more'n your father and mother," suggested Wade.

"I know who'll have to do all the work," the boy retorted, bitterness and rebellion in his tone.

"Oh, quit your arguin'," commanded the mother. "We got enough to do to move nearer that water tonight, without wastin' time talkin'. Supper's ready."

Martin and Nellie sat down beside the red-and-white-checkered cloth spread on the ground, and Wade, after passing the still fretting baby to his wife, took his place with them.

"Seems like he gets thinner every day," he commented, anxiously.

With a swift gesture of fierce tenderness, Mrs. Wade gathered little Benny to her. "Oh, God!" she gasped. "I know I'm goin' to lose him. That cow's milk don't set right on his stomach."

"It won't set any better after old Brindle fills up on this dust," observed Martin, belligerency in his brassy voice.

"That'll do," came sharply from his father. "I don't think this is paradise no more'n you do, but we wouldn't be the first who've come with nothing but a team and made a living. You mark what I tell you, Martin, land ain't always goin' to be had so cheap and I won't be living this time another year. Before I die, I'm goin' to see your mother and you children settled. Some day, when you've got a fine farm here, you'll see the sense of what I'm doin' now and thank me for it."

The boy's cold, blue eyes became the color of ice, as he retorted: "If I ever make a farm out o' this dust, I'll sure 'ave earned it."

"I guess your mother'll be doin' her share of that, all right. And don't you forget it."

As he intoned in even accents, Wade's eyes, so deep in their somber sockets, dwelt with a strange, wistful compassion on his faded wife. The rays of the setting sun brought out the drabness of her. Already, at thirty-five, grey streaked the scanty, dull hair, wrinkles lined the worn olive-brown face, and the tendons of the thin neck stood out. Chaotically, he compared her to the happy young girl - round of cheek and laughing of eye - he had married back in Ohio, fifteen years before. It comforted him a little to remember he hadn't done so badly by her until the war had torn him from his rented farm and she had been forced to do a man's work in field and barn. Exposure and a lung wound from a rebel bullet had sent Wade home an invalid, and during the five years which had followed, he had realized only too well how little help he had been to her.

It is not likely he would have had the iron persistency of purpose to drag her through this new stern trial if he had not known that in her heart, as in his, there gnawed ever an all-devouring hunger to work land of their own, a fervent aspiration to establish a solid basis of self-sustentation upon which their children might build. From the day a letter had come from Peter Mall, an ex-comrade in Wade's old regiment, saying the quarter-section next his own could be bought by paying annually a dollar and twenty-five cents an acre for seven years, their hopes had risen into determination that had become unshakable. Before the eyes of Jacob and Sarah Wade there had hovered, like a promise, the picture of the snug farm that could be evolved from this virgin soil. Strengthened by this vision and stimulated by the fact of Wade's increasing weakness, they had sold their few possessions, except the simplest necessities for camping, had made a canvas cover for their wagon, stocked up with smoked meat, corn meal and coffee, tied old Brindle behind, fastened a coop of chickens against the wagon-box and, without faltering, had made the long pilgrimage. Their indomitable courage and faith, Martin's physical strength and the pulling power of their two ring-boned horses - this was their capital.

It seemed pitifully meager to Wade at that despondent moment, exhausted as he was by the long, hard journey and the sultry heat. Never had he been so taunted by a sense of failure, so torn by the haunting knowledge that he must soon leave his family. To die - that was nothing; but the fears of what his death might mean to this group, gripped his heart and shook his soul.

If only Martin were more tender! There was something so ruthless in the boy, so overbearing and heartless. Not that he was ever deliberately cruel, but there was an insensibility to the feelings of others, a capacity placidly to ignore them, that made Wade tremble for the future. Martin would work, and work hard; he was no shirk, but would he ever feel any responsibility toward his younger brother and sister? Would he be loyal to his mother? Wade wondered if his wife ever felt as he did - almost afraid of this son of theirs. He had a way of making his father seem foolishly inexperienced and ineffectual.

"I reckon," Wade analysed laboriously, "it's because I'm gettin' less able all the time and he's growing so fast - him limber an' quick, and me all thumbs. There ain't nothing like just plain muscle and size to make a fellow feel as if he know'd it all."

Martin had never seemed more competent than this evening as, supper over, he harnessed the horses and helped his mother set the little caravan in motion. It was Martin who guided them to the creek, Martin who decided just where to locate their camp, Martin who, early the next morning, unloaded the wagon and made a temporary tent from its cover, and Martin who set forth on a saddleless horse in search of Peter Mall. When he returned, the big, kindly man came with him, and in Martin's arms there squealed and wriggled a shoat.

"A smart boy you've got, Jacob," chuckled Peter, jovially, after the first heart-warming greetings. "See that critter! Blame me if Martin, here, didn't speak right up and ask me to lend 'er to you!" And he collapsed into gargantuan laughter.

"I promised when she'd growed up and brought pigs, we'd give him back two for one," Martin hastily explained.

"That's what he said," nodded Peter, carefully switching his navy plug to the opposite cheek before settling down to reply, "and sez I, 'Why, Martin, what d'ye want o' that there shoat? You ain't got nothin' to keep her on!' 'If I can borrow the pig,' sez he, 'I reckon I can borrow the feed somewheres.' God knows, he'll find that ain't so plentiful, but he's got the right idea. A new country's a poor man's country and fellows like us have to stand together. It's borrow and lend out here. I know where you can get some seed wheat if you want to try puttin' it in this fall. There's a man by the name of Perry - lives just across the Missouri line - who has thrashed fifteen hundred bushel and he'll lend you three hundred or so. He's willing to take a chance, but if you get a crop he wants you should give him back an extra three hundred."

It was a hard bargain, but one that Wade could afford to take up, for if the wheat were to freeze out, or if the grasshoppers should eat it, or the chinch bugs ruin it, or a hail storm beat it down into the mud, or if any of the many hatreds Stepmother Nature holds out toward those trusting souls who would squeeze a living from her hard hands - if any of these misfortunes should transpire, he would be out nothing but labor, and that was the one thing he and Martin could afford to risk.

The seed deal was arranged, and Martin made the trip six times back and forth, for the wagon could hold only fifty bushels. Perry lived twenty miles from the Wades and a whole day was consumed with each load. It was evening when Martin, hungry and tired, reached home with the last one; and, as he stopped beside the tent, he noticed with surprise that there was no sign of cooking. Nellie was huddled against her mother, who sat, idle, with little Benny in her arms. The tragic yearning her whole body expressed, as she held the baby close, arrested the boy's attention, filled him with clamoring uneasiness. His father came to help him unhitch.

"What's the matter with Benny?"

Wade looked at Martin queerly. "He's dead. Died this mornin' and your ma's been holding him just like that. I want you should ride over to Peter's and see if you can fetch his woman."

"No!" came from Mrs. Wade, brokenly, "I don't want no one. Just let me alone."

The shattering anguish in his mother's voice startled Martin, stirred within him tumultuous, veiled sensations. He was unaccustomed to seeing her show suffering, and it embarrassed him. Restless and uncomfortable, he was glad when his father called him to help decide where to dig the grave, and fell the timber from which to make a rough box. From time to time, through the long night, he could not avoid observing his mother. In the white moonlight, she and Benny looked as if they had been carved from stone. Dawn was breaking over them when Wade, surrendering to a surge of pity, put his arms around her with awkward gentleness. "Ma, we got to bury 'im."

A low, half-suppressed sob broke from Mrs. Wade's tight lips as she clasped the tiny figure and pressed her cheek against the little head.

"I can't give him up," she moaned, "I can't! It wasn't so hard with the others. Their sickness was the hand of God, but Benny just ain't had enough to eat. Seems like it'll kill me."

With deepened discomfort, Martin hurried to the creek to water the horses. It was good, he felt, to have chores to do. This knowledge shot through him with the same thrill of discovery that a man enjoys when he first finds what an escape from the solidity of fact lies in liquor. If one worked hard and fast one could forget. That was what work did. It made one forget - that moan, that note of agony in his mother's voice, that hurt look in her eyes, that bronze group in the moonlight. By the time he had finished his chores, his mother was getting breakfast as usual. With unspeakable relief, Martin noticed that though pain haunted her face, she was not crying.

"I heard while I was over in Missouri, yesterday," he ventured, "of a one-room house down in the Indian Territory. The fellow who built it's give up and gone back East. Maybe we could fix a sledge and haul it up here."

"I ain't got the strength to help," said Wade.

Martin's eyes involuntarily sought his mother's. He knew the power in her lean, muscular arms, the strength in her narrow shoulders.

"We'd better fetch it," she agreed.

The pair made the trip down on horseback and brought back the shack that was to be home for many years. Eighteen miles off a man had some extra hand-cut shingles which he was willing to trade for a horse-collar. While Mrs. Wade took the long drive Martin, under his father's guidance, chopped down enough trees to build a little lean-to kitchen and make-shift stable. Sixteen miles south another neighbor had some potatoes to exchange for a hatching of chickens. Martin rode over with the hen and her downy brood. The long rides, consuming hours, were trying, for Martin was needed every moment on a farm where everything was still to be done.

Day by day Wade was growing weaker, and it was Mrs. Wade who helped put in the crop, borrowing a plow, harrow, and extra team, and repaying the loan with the use of their own horses and wagon. Luck was with their wheat, which soon waved green. It seemed one of life's harsh jests that now, when the tired, ill-nourished baby had fretted his last, old Brindle, waxing fat and sleek on the wheat pasture, should give more rich cream than the Wades could use. "He could have lived on the skimmed milk we feed to the pigs," thought Martin.

In the Spring he went with his father into Fallon, the nearest trading point, to see David Robinson, the owner of the local bank. By giving a chattel mortgage on their growing wheat, they borrowed enough, at twenty per cent, to buy seed corn and a plow. It was Wade's last effort. Before the corn was in tassel, he had been laid beside Benny.

Martin, who already had been doing a man's work, now assumed a man's responsibilities. Mrs. Wade consulted more and more with him, relied more and more upon his judgment. She was immensely proud of him, of his steadiness and dependability, but at rare moments, remembering her own normal childhood, she would think with compunction: "It ain't right. Young 'uns ought to have some fun. Seems like it's makin' him too old for his age." She never spoke of these feelings, however. There were no expressions of tenderness in the Wade household. She was doing her best by her children and they knew it. Even Nellie, child that she was, understood the grimness of the battle before them.

They were able to thresh enough wheat to repay their debt of six hundred bushels and keep an additional three hundred of seed for the following year. The remaining seven hundred and fifty they sold at twenty-five cents a bushel by hauling them to Fort Scott - thirty miles distant. Each trip meant ten dollars, but to the Wades, to whom this one hundred and eighty-seven dollars - the first actual money they had seen in over a year - was a fortune, these journeys were rides of triumph, fugitive flashes of glory in the long, gray struggle.

That Fall they paid the first installment of two hundred dollars on their land and Martin persuaded his mother to give and Robinson to take a chattel on their two horses, old Brindle, her calf and the pigs, that other much-needed implements might be bought. Mrs. Wade toiled early and late, doing part of the chores and double her share of the Spring plowing that Martin, as well as Nellie, could attend school in Fallon.

"I don't care about goin'," he had protested squirmingly.

But on this matter his mother was without compromise. "Don't say that," she had commanded, her voice shaken and her eyes bright with the intensity of her emotion; "you're goin' to get an education."

And Martin, surprised and embarrassed by his mother's unusual exhibition of feeling, had answered, roughly: "Aw, well, all right then. Don't take on. I didn't say I wouldn't, did I?"

He was twenty-three and Nellie sixteen when, worn out and broken down before her time, her resistance completely undermined, Mrs. Wade died suddenly of pneumonia. Within the year Nellie married Bert Mall, Peter's eldest son, and Martin, at once, bought out her half interest in the farm, stock and implements, giving a first mortgage to Robinson in order to pay cash.

"I'm making it thirty dollars an acre," he explained.

"That's fair," conceded the banker, "though the time will come when it will be cheap at a hundred and a half. There's coal under all this county, millions of dollars' worth waiting to be mined."

"Maybe," assented Martin, laconically.

As he sat in the dingy, little backroom of the bank, while Robinson's pen scratched busily drawing up the papers, he was conscious of an odd thrill. The land - it was all his own! But with this thrill welled a wave of resentment over what he considered a preposterous imposition. Who had made the land into a farm? What had Nellie ever put into it that it should be half hers? His mother - now, that was different. She and he had toiled side by side like real partners; her efforts had been real and unstinted. If he were buying her out, for instance - but Nellie! Well, that was the way, he noticed, with many women - doing little and demanding much. He didn't care for them; not he. From the day Nellie left, Martin managed alone in the shack, "baching it," and putting his whole heart and soul into the development of his quarter-section.

II

OUT OF THE DUST

AT thirty-four, Martin was still unmarried, and though he had not travelled far on that strange road to affluence which for some seems a macadamized boulevard, but for so many, like himself, a rough cow-path, he had done better than the average farmer of Fallon County. To be sure, this was nothing over which to gloat. A man who received forty cents a bushel for wheat was satisfied; corn sold at twenty-eight cents, and the hogs it fattened in proportion. But his hundred and sixty acres were clear from debt, four thousand dollars were on deposit drawing three per cent in The First State Bank - the old Bank of Fallon, now incorporated with Robinson as its president. In the pasture, fourteen sows with their seventy-five spring pigs rooted beside the sleek herd of steers fattening for market; the granary bulged with corn; two hundred bushels of seed wheat were ready for sowing; his machinery was in excellent condition; his four Percheron mares brought him, each, a fine mule colt once a year; and the well never went dry, even in August. Martin was - if one discounted the harshness of the life, the dirt, the endless duties and the ever-pressing chores - a Kansas plutocrat.

One fiery July day, David Robinson drew up before Martin's shack. The little old box-house was still unpainted without and unpapered within. Two chairs, a home-made table with a Kansas City Star as a cloth, a sheetless bed, a rough cupboard, a stove and floors carpeted with accumulations of untidiness completed the furnishings.

"Chris-to-pher Columbus!" exploded Robinson, "why don't you fix yourself up a bit, Martin? The Lord knows you're going to be able to afford it. What you need is a wife - someone to look after you." And as Martin, observing him calmly, made no response, he added, "I suppose you know what I want. You've been watching for this day, eh, Martin? All Fallon County's sitting on its haunches - waiting."

"Oh, I haven't been worrying. A fellow situated like me, with a hundred and sixty right in the way of a coal company, can afford to be independent."

"You understand our procedure, Martin," Robinson continued. "We are frank and aboveboard. We set the price, and if you can't see your way clear to take it there are no hard feelings. We simply call it off - for good."

Wade knew how true this was. When the mining first began, several rebels toward the East had tried profitlessly to buck this irrefragable game and had found they had battered their unyielding heads against an equally unyielding stone wall. These men had demanded more and Robinson's company, true to its threat, had urbanely gone around their farms, travelled on and left them behind, their coal untouched and certain to so remain. Such inelastic lessons, given time to soak in, were sobering.

"Now," said Robinson, in his amiable matter-of-fact manner, "as I happen to know the history of this quarter, backwards and forwards, we can do up this deal in short order. You sign this contract, which is exactly like all the others we use, and I'll hand over your check. We get the bottom; you keep the top; I give you the sixteen thousand, and the thing is done."

"Well, Martin," he added, genially, as Wade signed his name, "it's a long day since you came in with your father to make that first loan to buy seed corn. Wouldn't he have opened his eyes if any one had prophesied this? It's a pity your mother couldn't have lived to enjoy your good fortune. A fine, plucky woman, your mother. They don't make many like her."

Long after Robinson's buggy was out of sight, Martin stood in his doorway and stared at the five handsome figures, spelled out the even more convincing words and admired the excellent reproduction of The First State Bank.

"This is a whole lot of money," his thoughts ran. "I'm rich. All this land still mine - practically as much mine as ever - all this stock and twenty thousand dollars in money - in cash. It's a fact. I, Martin Wade, am rich."

He remembered how he had exulted, how jubilant, even intoxicated, he had felt when he had received the ten dollars for the first load of wheat he had hauled to Fort Scott. Now, with a check for sixteen thousand - SIXTEEN THOUSAND DOLLARS! - in his hand, he stood dumbly, curiously unmoved.

Slowly, the first bitter months on this land, little Benny's death from lack of nourishment, his father's desperate efforts to establish his family, the years of his mother's slow crucifixion, his own long struggle - all floated before him in a fog of reverie. Years of deprivation, of bending toil and then, suddenly, this had come - this miracle symbolized by this piece of paper. Martin moistened his lips. Mentally, he realized all the dramatic significance of what had happened, but it gave him none of the elation he had expected.

This bewildered and angered him. Sixteen thousand dollars and with it no thrill. What was lacking? As he pondered, puzzled and disappointed, it came to him that he needed something by which to measure his wealth, someone whose appreciation of it would make it real to him, give him a genuine sense of its possession. What if he were to take Robinson's advice: fix up a bit and - marry?

Nellie had often urged the advantages of this, but he had never had much to do with women; they did not belong in his world and he had not missed them; he had never before felt a need of marriage. Upon the few occasions when, driven by his sister's persistence, he had vaguely considered it, he had shrunk away quickly from the thought of the unavoidable changes which would be ushered in by such a step. This shack, itself - no one whom he would want would, in this day, consent to live in it, and, if he should marry, his wife must be a superior woman, good looking, and with the push and energy of his mother. He thought of all she had meant to his father; and there was Nellie, not to be spoken of in the same breath, yet making Bert Mall a good wife. What a cook she was! Memories of her hot, fluffy biscuits, baked chicken, apple pies and delicious coffee, carried trailing aromas that set his nostrils twitching. It would be pleasant to have satisfying meals once more, to be relieved, too, of the bother of the three hundred chickens, to have some one about in the evenings. True, there would be expense, oh, such expense - the courting, the presents, the wedding, the building, the furniture, and, later, innumerable new kinds of bills. But weren't all the men around him married? Surely, if they, not nearly as well off as himself, could afford it, so could he.

Besides, wasn't it all different now that he held this check in his hand? These sixteen thousand dollars were not the same dollars which he had extorted from close-fisted Nature. Each of those had come so lamely, was such a symbol of sweat and aching muscles, that to spend one was like parting with a portion of himself, but this new, almost incredible fortune, had come without a turn of his hand, without an hour's labor. To Martin, the distinction was sharp and actual.

He figured quickly. Five thousand dollars would do wonders. With that amount, he would build so substantially that his neighbors could no longer feel the disapprobation in which, according to Nellie, he was beginning to be held, because of his sordid, hermit-like life. That five thousand could buy many cows and additional acreage - but just now a home and a wife would be better investments. Yes, he would marry and a house should be his bait. That was settled. He would drive into Fallon at once to see the carpenter and deposit the check.

He was already out of the house when a thought struck him. Suppose he were to meet just the woman he might want? These soiled, once-blue overalls, these heavy, manure-spotted shoes, this greasy, shapeless straw hat, with its dozen matches showing their red heads over the band, the good soils and fertilizers of Kansas resting placidly in his ears and the lines of his neck - such a Romeo might not tempt his Juliet; he must spruce up.

On an aged soap-box behind the house, several inches of grey water in a battered tin-pan indicated a previous effort. He tossed the greasy liquid to the ground and from the well, near the large, home-built barn, refilled the make-shift basin. Martin's ablutions were always a strenuous affair. In his cupped hands he brought the water toward his face and, at the moment he was about to apply it, made pointless attempts to blow it away. This blowing and sputtering indicated the especial importance of an occasion - the more important, the more vigorously he blew. Today, the cold water gave a healthy glow to his face, which, after much stropping of his razor, he shaved of a week's growth of beard, tawny as his thick, crisp hair where the sun had not yet bleached it. This, he soaked thoroughly, in lieu of brushing, before using a crippled piece of comb. The dividing line between washed and unwashed was one inch above his neckband and two above his wrists. Even when fresh from a scrubbing, his hands were not entirely clean. They had been so long in contact with the earth that it had become absorbed into the very pores of his skin; but they were powerful hands, interesting, with long palms and spatulate fingers. The black strips at the end of each nail, Martin pared off with his jackknife.

He entered the house a trifle nervously, positive that his only clean shirt, at present spread over his precious shot-gun, had been worn once more than he could have wished, but, after all, how much of one's shirt showed? It would pass. The coat-shirt not yet introduced, a man had to slip the old-fashioned kind over his head, drag it down past his shoulders and poke blindly for the sleeve openings. Martin was thankful when he felt the collar buttons in their holes. His salt and pepper suit was of a stiff, unyielding material, and the first time he had worn it the creases had vanished never to return. Before putting on his celluloid collar, he spat on it and smeared it off with the tail of his shirt. A recalcitrant metal shaper insisted on peeking from under his lapels, and his ready-made tie with its two grey satin-covered cardboard wings pushed out of sight, see-sawed, necessitating frequent adjustments. His brown derby, the rim of which made almost three quarters of a circle at each side, seemed to want to get as far as possible from his ears and, at the same time, remain perched on his head. The yellow shoes looked as though each had half a billiard ball in the toe, and the entire tops were perforated with many diverging lines in an attempt for the decorative. Those were the days of sore feet and corns! Hart Schaffner and Marx had not yet become rural America's tailor. Sartorial magicians in Chicago had not yet won over the young men of the great corn belt, with their snappy lines and style for the millions. In 1890, when a suit served merely as contrast to a pair of overalls, the Martin Wades who would clothe themselves pulled their garments from the piles on long tables. It was for the next generation to patronize clothiers who kept each suit on its separate hanger. A moving-picture of the tall, broad-shouldered fellow, as, with creaking steps, he walked from the house, might bring a laugh from the young farmers of this more fastidious day, but Martin was dressed no worse than any of his neighbors and far better than many. Health, vigor, sturdiness, self-reliance shone from him, and once his make-up had ceased to obtrude its clumsiness, he struck one as handsome. His was a commanding physique, hard as the grim plains from which he wrested his living.

As Martin drove into Fallon, his attention was directed toward the architecture and the women. He observed that the average homes were merely a little larger than his own - four, six, or eight rooms instead of one, made a little trimmer with neat porches and surrounded by well-cut lawns, instead of weeds. He, with his new budget, could do better. Even Robinson's well-constructed residence had probably cost only three thousand more than he himself planned to spend. Its suggestion of originality had been all but submerged by carpenters spoiled through constant work on commonplace buildings. But to Martin it was a marvellous mansion. He told himself that with such a place moved out to his quarter-section, he could have stood on his door-step and chosen whomever he wished for a wife.

It was an elemental materialism, difficult to understand, but it was a language very clear to Martin. Marriage with the men and women of his world was a practical business, arranged and conducted by practical people, who lived practical lives, and died practical deaths. The women who might pass his way could deny their lust for concrete possessions, but their actions, however concealed their motives, would give the lie to any ineffectual glamour of romance they might attempt to fling over their carefully measured adventures of the heart.

Martin smiled cynically as he let his thoughts drift along this channel. "What a lot of bosh is talked about lovers," his comment ran. "As if everyone didn't really know how much like drunken men they are - saying things which in a month they'll have forgotten. Folks pretend to approve of 'em and all the while they're laughing at 'em up their sleeves. But how they respect a man who's got the root they're all grubbing for! It may be the root of all evil, but it's a fact that everything people want grows from it. They hate a man for having it, but they'd like to be him. Their hearts have all got strings dangling from 'em, especially the women's. A house tied onto the other end ought to be hefty enough to fetch the best of the lot."

Who could she be, anyway? Was she someone in Fallon? He drove slowly, thinking over the families in the different houses - four to each side of the block. The street, even yet, was little more than a country road. There was no indication of the six miles of pavement which later were to be Fallon's pride. It had rained earlier in the week and Martin was obliged to be careful of the chuck-holes in the sticky, heavy gumbo soon to be the bane of pioneers venturing forth in what were to be known for a few short years as "horseless carriages."

Bumping along he recalled to his mind the various girls with whom he had gone to school. As if the sight of the building, itself, would sharpen his memory, he turned north and drove past it. Like its south, east and west counterparts, it was a solid two-story brick affair. In time it would be demolished to make way for what would be known as the "Emerson School," in which, to be worthy of this high title, the huge stoves would be supplanted with hot-water pipes, oil lamps with soft, indirect lighting, and unsightly out-buildings with modern plumbing. The South building would become the "Whittier School," the East, the "Longfellow," and the West, not to be neglected by culture's invasion, the "Oliver Wendell Holmes." But these changes were still to be effected. Many a school board meeting was first to be split into stormy factions of conservatives fighting to hold the old, and of anarchists threatening civilization with their clamors for experimentation. Many a bond election was yet to rip the town in two, with the retired farmers, whose children were grown and through school, satisfied with things as they were and parents of the new generation demanding gymnasiums, tennis courts, victrolas, domestic science laboratories, a public health nurse and individual lockers. Yes, and the faddists were to win despite the other side's incontrovertible evidence that Fallon was headed for bankruptcy and that the proposed bonds and outstanding ones could never be met.

Martin drove, meditatively, around the school-house and was still engrossed in the problem of "Who?" when he reached the Square. The neat canvas drops of later years had not yet replaced the wooden awnings which gave to the town such a decidedly western appearance and which threw the sidewalks and sheltered windows into deep pools of shadow. The old brick store-building which housed The First State Bank was like a cool cavern. He brought out the check quietly but with a full consciousness that with one gesture he was shoving enough over that scratched and worn walnut counter to buy out half the bank.

James Osborne, the youthful cashier, feigned complete paralysis.

"Why don't you give a poor fellow some warning?" he beamed good-naturedly, "or maybe you think you've strayed into Wall Street. This is Fallon. Fallon, Kansas. So you've had your merry little session with Robinson? Put it here!" and he extended a cordial hand.

"Oh, considering the wait, it isn't so wonderful. Sixteen thousand is an awful lot when it's coming, but it just seems about half as big when it gets here."

Martin was talking not so much for Osborne's benefit as to impress a woman who had entered behind him and was awaiting her turn. He wondered why, in his mental quest, he had not thought of her. Here was the very person for whom he was looking. Rose Conroy, the editor of the better local weekly, a year or so younger than himself, pleasant, capable. Here was a real woman, one above the average in character and brains.

With a quick glance he took in her well-built figure. Everything about Rose - every line, every tone of her coloring suggested warmth, generosity, bigness. She was as much above medium height for a woman as Martin for a man. About her temples the line of her bright golden-brown hair had an oddly pleasing irregularity. The rosy color in her cheeks brought out the rich creamy whiteness of her skin. Warm, gray-blue eyes were set far apart beneath a kind, broad forehead and her wide, generous mouth seemed made to smile. The impression of good temper and fun was accented by her nose, ever so slightly up-tilted. Some might have thought Rose too large, her hips too rounded, the soft deep bosom too full, but Martin's eyes were approving. Even her hands, plump, with broad palms, square fingers and well-kept nails, suggested decision. He felt the quiet distinction of her simple white dress. She was like a full-blown, luxuriant white and gold flower - like a rose, a full-blown white rose, Martin realized, suddenly. One couldn't call her pretty, but there was something about her that gave the impression of sumptuous good looks. He liked, too, the spirited carriage of her head. "Healthy, good-sense, sound all through," was his final appraisement.

Pocketing his bank-book, he gave her a sharp nod, a colorless "how-de-do, Miss Rose," and a tip of the hat that might have been a little less stiff had he been more accustomed to greeting the ladies. "Right well, thank you, Martin," was her cordial response, and her friendly smile told him she had heard and understood the remarks about the big deal. He was curious to know how it had impressed her.

Hurrying out, he asked himself how he could begin advances. Either he must do something quickly in time to get home for the evening chores or he must wait until another day. He must think out a plan, at once. Passing the bakery, half way down the block, he dropped in, ordered a chocolate ice-cream soda, and chose a seat near the window. As he had expected, it was not long before he saw Rose go across the courthouse yard toward her office on the north side of the square. He liked the swift, easy way in which she walked. She had been walking the first time he had ever seen her, thirteen years before, when her father had led his family uptown from the station, the day of their arrival in Fallon.

Patrick Conroy had come from Sharon, Illinois, to perform the thankless task of starting a weekly newspaper in a town already undernourishing one. By sheer stubbornness he had at last established it. Twelve hundred subscribers, their little printing jobs, advertisers who bought liberal portions of space at ten cents an inch - all had enabled him to give his children a living that was a shade better than an existence. He had died less than a year ago, and Martin, like the rest of the community, had supposed the Fallon Independent would be sold or suspended. Instead, as quietly and matter-of-factly as she had filled her dead mother's place in the home while her brothers and sisters were growing up, Rose stepped into her father's business, took over the editorship and with a boy to do the typesetting and presswork, continued the paper without missing an issue. It even paid a little better than before, partly because it flattered Fallon's sense of Christian helpfulness to throw whatever it could in Rose's way, but chiefly because she made the Independent a livelier sheet with double the usual number of "Personals."

Yes, decidedly, Rose had force and push. Martin's mind was made up. He would drop into the Independent ostensibly to extend his subscription, but really to get on more intimate terms with the woman whom he had now firmly determined should become his wife. He drew a deep breath of relaxation and finished the glass of sweetness with that sense of self-conscious sheepishness which most men feel when they surrender to the sticky charms of an ice-cream soda. A few minutes later he stood beside Rose's worn desk.

"How-do-you-do, once more, Miss Rose of Sharon. You're not the Bible's Rose of Sharon, are you?" he joshed a bit awkwardly.

"If I were a rose of anywhere, I'd soon wilt in this stuffy little office of inky smells," she answered pleasantly. "A rose would need petals of leather to get by here."

"A rose, by rights, belongs out of doors," - Martin indicated the direction of his farm - "out there where the sun shines and there's no smells except the rich, healthy smells of nature."

A merry twinkle appeared in Rose's eyes. "Aren't roses out there" - and her gesture was in the same direction - "rather apt to be crowded down by the weeds?"

"Not if there was a good strong man about - a man who

wanted to cultivate the soil and give the rose a pretty place in which to bloom."

"Why, Martin," Rose laughed lightly, "the way you're fixed out there with that shack, the only thing that ever blooms is a fine crop of rag-weeds."

At this gratuitous thrust a flood of crimson surged up Martin's magnificent, column-like throat and broke in hot waves over his cheeks. "Well, it's not going to be that way for long," he announced evenly. "I'm going to plant a rose - a real rose there soon and everything is going to be right - garden, house and all."

"Is this your way of telling me you're going to be married?"

"Kinda. The only trouble is, I haven't got my rose yet."

"Well, if I can't have that item, at least I can print something about the selling of your coal rights. People will be interested because it shows the operators are coming in our direction. Here in Fallon, we can hardly realize all that this sudden new promotion may mean. From that conversation I heard at the bank I guess you got the regulation hundred an acre."

"Yes, and a good part of it is going into a first-class modern house with a heating plant and running hot and cold water in a tiled-floor bath-room, and a concrete cellar for the woman's preserved things and built-in cupboards, lots of closets, a big garret, and hardwood floors and fancy paper on the walls, and the prettiest polished golden oak furniture you can buy in Kansas City, not to mention a big fireplace and wide, sunny porches. A rose ought to be happy in a garden like that, don't you think? Folks'll say I've gone crazy when they see my building spree, but I know what I'm about. It's time I married and the woman who decides to be my wife is going to be glad to stay with me - "

"See here, Martin Wade, what ARE you driving at? What does

all this talk mean anyway? Do you want me to give you a boost with someone?"

"You've hit it."

"Who is she?" Rose asked, with genuine curiosity.

"You," he said bluntly.

"Well, of all the proposals!"

"There's nothing to beat around the bush about. I'm only thirty-four, a hard worker, with a tidy sum to boot - not that I'm boasting about it."

"But, Martin, what makes you think I could make you happy?"

Martin felt embarrassed. He was not looking for happiness but merely for more of the physical comforts, and an escape from loneliness. He was practical; he fancied he knew about what could be expected from marriage, just as he knew exactly how many steers and hogs his farm could support. This was a new idea - happiness. It had never entered into his calculations. Life as he knew it was hard. There was no happiness in those fields when burned by the hot August winds, the soil breaking into cakes that left crevices which seemed to groan for water. That sky with its clouds that gave no rain was a hard sky. The people he knew were sometimes contented, but he could not remember ever having known any to whom the word "happy" could be applied. His father and mother - they had been a good husband and wife. But happy? They had been far too absorbed in the bitter struggle for a livelihood to have time to think of happiness. This had been equally true of the elder Malls, was true today of Nellie and her husband. A man and a woman needed each other's help, could make a more successful fight, go farther together than either could alone. To Martin that was the whole matter in a nutshell, and Rose's gentle question threw him into momentary confusion.

"I don't know," he answered uneasily. "We both like to make a success of things and we'd have plenty to do with. We'd make a pretty good pulling team."

Rose considered this thoughtfully. "Perhaps the people who work together best are the happiest. But somehow I'd never pictured myself on a farm."

"Of course, I don't expect you to make up your mind right away," Martin conceded. "It's something to study over. I'll come around to your place tomorrow evening after I get the chores done up and we can talk some more."

So far as Martin was concerned, the matter was clinched. He felt not the slightest doubt but that it was merely a question of time before Rose would consent to his proposition.

After he had left, she reviewed it a little sadly. It wasn't the kind of marriage of which she had always dreamed. She realized that she was capable of profound devotion, of responding with her whole being to a deep love. But was it probable that this love would ever come? She thought over the men of Fallon and its neighborhood. There were few as handsome as Martin - not one with such generous plans. She knew her own domestic talents. She was a born housekeeper and home-maker. It had been a curious destiny that had driven her into a newspaper office, and at that very moment, there lay on her desk, like a whisper from Fate, the written offer from the rival paper to buy her out for fifteen hundred dollars, giving herself a position on the consolidated staff. She had been pondering over this proposal when Martin interrupted her.

It wasn't as if she were younger or likely to start somewhere else. She would live out her life in Fallon, that she knew. There was little chance of her meeting new men, and those established enough to make marriage with them desirable were already married. Candidly, she admitted that if she turned Martin Wade down now, she might never have another such opportunity. If only she could feel that he cared for her - loved her. But wasn't the fact that he was asking her to be his wife proof of that? It was very strange. She had never suspected that Martin had ever felt drawn to her. With a sigh she pressed her large, capable hands to her heart. Its deep piercing ache brought tears to her eyes. She felt, bitterly, that she was being cheated of too much that was sweet and precious - it was all wrong - she would be making a mistake. For a moment, she was overwhelmed. Then the practical common sense that had been instilled into her from her earliest consciousness, even as it had been instilled into Martin, reasserted itself. After all, perhaps he was right - the busy people were the happy people. Many couples who began marriage madly in love ended in the divorce courts. Martin was kind and it would be wonderful to have the home he had described. She imagined herself mistress of it, thrilled with the warm hospitality she would radiate, entertained already at missionary meetings and at club. At least, she would be less lonely. It would be a fuller life than now. What was she getting, really getting, alone, out of this world? She and Martin would be good partners. Poor boy! What a long, hard, cheerless existence he had led. Tenderness welled in her heart and stilled its pain. Perhaps his emotions were far deeper than he could express in words. His way was to plan for her comfort. Wasn't there something big about his simple cards-on-the-table wooing? And he had called her his rose, his Rose of Sharon. The new house was to be the garden in which she should blossom. To be sure, he had said it all awkwardly, but Rose, who was devout, knew the stately Song of Solomon and as she recalled the magnificent outburst of passion she almost let herself be convinced that Martin was a poet-lover in the rough.

And all the while, giving pattern to her flying thoughts, the contents of a letter, received the day before, echoed through her mind. Her sister, Norah, the youngest of the family, had told of her first baby. "We have named her for you, darling," she wrote. "Oh, Rose, she has brought me such deep happiness. I wonder if this ecstasy can last. Her little hand against my breast - it is so warm and soft - like a flower's curling petal, as delicate and as beautiful as a butterfly's wing. I never knew until now what life really meant." As Rose reread the throbbing lines and pictured the eager-eyed young mother, her own sweet face glowed with reflected joy and with the knowledge that this ecstasy, this deeper understanding could come to her, too - Martin, he was vigorous, so worthy of being the father of her children. He would love them, of course, and provide for them better than any other man she knew. Had not Norah married a plain farmer who was only a tenant? The new little Rose's father was not to be compared to Martin, and yet he had brought the supreme experience to her sister. So Rose sat dreaming, the arid level of monotonous days which, one short hour ago, had stretched before her, flowering into fragrant, sun-filled fields.

Meanwhile, Martin congratulated himself upon having found a woman as sensible, industrious and free from foolish notions, as even he could wish.

III

DUST IN HER HEART

SIX weeks later Martin and Rose were married. Martin had let the contract for the new house and barn to Silas Fletcher, Fallon's leading carpenter, who had the science of construction reduced to utter simplicity. He had listened to Martin's description of what he wished and, after some rough figuring, had proceeded to draw the plans on the back of a large envelope. Both Rose and Martin knew that those rude lines would serve unfailingly. For three thousand dollars Fletcher would build the very house Martin had pictured to Rose: a two-story one with four nice rooms and a bath upstairs, four rooms and a pantry downstairs, a floored garret, concrete cellar, an inviting fireplace and wide porches. For two thousand dollars he would give a substantial barn capable of holding a hundred tons of hay and of accommodating twenty cows and four horses.

Rose had been deeply touched by the thoroughness of Martin's plans, by his unfailing consideration for her comfort. True, there had been moments when her warm, loving nature had been chilled. At such times, misgivings had clamored and she had, finally, all but made up her mind to tell him that she could not go on - that it had all been a mistake. She would say to him, she had decided: "Martin, you are one of the kindest and best men, and I could be happy with you if only you loved me, but you don't really care for me and you never will. I feel it. Oh, I do! and I could not bear it - to live with you day in and day out and know that."

But she had reckoned without her own goodness of heart. On the very evening on which she had quite determined to tell Martin this decision he also had arrived at one. As soon as he had entered Rose's little parlor he had exclaimed with an enthusiasm unusual with him: "We broke the ground for your new garden, today, Rose of Sharon, and Fletcher wants to see you. There are some more little things you'll have to talk over with him. He understands that you're the one I want suited."

Rose had felt suddenly reassured. Why, she had asked herself contritely, couldn't she let Martin express his love in his own way? Why was she always trying to measure his feelings for her by set standards?

"I've been wondering," he had gone on quickly, "what you would think of putting up with my old shack while the new house is being built? It wouldn't be as if you were going to live there for long and you'd be right on hand to direct things."

"Why, I could do that, of course," she had answered pleasantly. "If you've lived there all these years, I surely ought to be able to live there a few months, but Martin - "

"I know what you're going to say," he had interrupted hastily. "You think we ought to wait a while longer, but if we're going to pull together for the rest of our lives why mightn't we just as well begin now? Why is one time any better than another?"

There had been a wistfulness, so rarely in Martin's voice, that Rose had detected it instantly. After all, why should she keep him waiting when he needed her so much, she had thought tenderly, all the sweet womanliness in her astir with yearnings to lift the cloud of loneliness from his life.

Rose had always believed love a breath of beauty that would hold its purity even in a hovel, but she had not been prepared for the sordidness that seemed to envelop her as she crossed the threshold of the first home of her married life. Martin, held in the clutch of the strained embarrassment that invariably laid its icy fingers around his heart whenever he found himself confronted by emotion, had suggested that Rose go in while he put up the horse and fed the stock. "Don't be scared if you find it pretty rough," he had warned, to which her light answer had lilted back, "Oh, I shan't mind."

And, as she stood in the doorway a moment later, her eyes taking in one by one, the murky windows, the dirty floor, the unwashed dishes, the tumbled bed, the rusty, grease bespattered stove choked with cold ashes, she told herself hotly that it was not the dirt nor even the desperate crassness that was smothering her joy. It was the fact that there was nowhere a touch to suggest preparation for her home-coming. Martin had made not even the crudest attempt to welcome her. It would have been as easy for Rose to be cheerful in the midst of mere squalor as for a flower to bloom white in a crowded tenement, but at the swift realization of the lack of tenderness for her which this indifference to her first impressions so clearly expressed, her faith in the man she had married began to wither. He had failed her in the very quality in which she had put her trust. Already, he had carelessly dropped the thoughtfulness by which he had won her. She wondered how she could have made herself believe that Martin loved her. "He has tried so hard in every way to show me how much I would mean to him," she justified herself. "But now he has me he just doesn't care what I think."

As Rose forced herself to face this squarely, something within her crumpled. Grim truth leered at her, hurling dust on her bright wings of illusion, poking cruel jests. "This is your wedding day," it taunted, "that tall figure out there near the dilapidated barn feeding his hogs is your husband. Oh, first, sweet, most precious hours! How you will always like to remember them! Here in this dirty shanty you will enter into love's fulfillment. How romantic! Why doesn't your heart leap and your arms ache for your new passion?" Tears pushed against her eyelids. Her new life was not going to be happy. Of this she was suddenly, irrevocably certain.

Rose struggled against a complete break-down. This was no time for a scene. What was the matter with her, anyway? Of course, Martin had not meant to disappoint her, nor deliberately hurt her. He probably thought this first home so temporary it didn't count. She simply would not mope. Of that she was positive, and a brave little smile swimming up from her troubled heart, she set about, with much energy, to achieve order, valiantly fighting back her insistent tears as she worked.

Meanwhile, Martin, totally oblivious of any cause for storm, was making trips to and from the barrel which contained shorts mixed with water' skimmed milk and house slops, the screaming, scrambling shoats gulping the pork-making mixture as rapidly as he could fetch it. He worked unconsciously, thinking, typically, not of Rose's reaction to this new life, but of what it held in store for himself.

He glanced toward the shack. Already the mere fact of a woman's presence beneath its roof seemed, to him, to give it a different aspect. Through the open door he observed that Rose was sweeping. How he had always hated the thought of any one handling what was his! He dumped another bucket of slops into the home-made trough. Why couldn't she just let things alone and get supper quietly? Heaven only knew what he had gotten himself into! But of one thing he was miserably certain; never again would he have that comfortable seclusion to which he had grown so accustomed. He had known this would be true, but the sight of Rose and her broom brought the realization of it home to him with an all too irritating vividness. Yes, everything was going to be different. There would be many changes and he would never know what to expect next. Why had he brought this upon himself; had he not lived alone for years? He had let the habit of obtaining whatever he started after get the better of him. Even today he could have drawn back from this marriage. But, he had sensed that Rose was about to do so herself, and this knowledge had pushed his determination to the final notch.

Martin shook his head ruefully. "This is 'The Song of Songs,'" he smiled, "and there is my Rose of Sharon. Guess I was never intended for a Solomon." Now that she was so close to him, in the very core of his life, this woman frightened him; instead of desire, there was dread. He wished Rose had been a man that he might go into that shack and eat ham and eggs with him while they talked crops and politics and animals. There would be no thrills in this opening chapter and he, if not his wife, would be shaken.

Martin was mental, an incurable individualist who found himself sufficient unto himself. He was different from his neighbors in that he was always thinking, asking questions and pondering over his conclusions. He had convinced himself that each demand of the body was useless except the food that nourished it, the clothes that warmed it and the sleep that repaired it. He hated soft things and the twist in his mind that was Martin proved to him their futility. Love? It was an empty dream, a shell that fooled. Its joys were fleeting. There was but one thing worth while and that was work. The body was made for it - the thumb to hold the hammer, the hand to pump the water and drive the horses, the legs to follow the plow, herd the cattle and chase the pigs from the cornfield, the ears to listen for strange noises from the stock, the eyes to watch for weeds and discover the lice on the hens, the mouth to yell the food call to the calves, the back to carry the bran. Work meant money, and money meant - what? It was merely a stick that measured the amount of work done. Then why did he toil so hard and save so scrupulously? His answer was always another question. What was there in life that could enable one to forget it faster? That woman in there waiting for him - oh, she would suffer before she realized the truth of this lesson he had already learned, and Martin felt a little pity for her.

When he went in for supper, Rose was just beginning to prepare it. With a catch of anger in his manner, he gave her a sharp look and saw that she had been crying. He couldn't remember ever before having had to deal with a weeping woman; even when Benny had died and his mother had been so shaken she had not given way to tears; so this was to be another of the new experiences which must trot in with marriage. It annoyed him.

"What's the matter, Rose?"

"Nothing at all, Martin."

"Nothing? You don't cry about nothing, do you?"

"No." Rose felt a sudden fear; she sensed a lack of pity in Martin, an unwillingness even to try to understand her conflicting emotions.

"Then you're crying about something. What is it?" There was command in his question. Martin was losing patience. He knew tears were used as weapons by women, but why in the world should Rose need any sort of weapon on the first day of their marriage? He hadn't done anything to her, said anything unkind. Was she going to be unreasonable? Now he was sure it was all wrong.

"What's the matter?" he demanded, his voice rising.

"Nothing's the matter. I'm just a little nervous." Rose began to cry afresh. If only Martin had come to her and put his arms around her, she would have been able to throw off her newly-born fear of him and this disheartening shattering of her faith in his kindness. But he was going to the other extreme, growing harder as she was becoming more panicky.

"Nervous? What's there to be nervous about?" Rose's answer was stifled sobbing. "You're not sorry you married today, I hope?" She shook her head. "Then what's this mean, anyway?"

"I was wondering if we are going to be happy after all - "

"Happy? You don't like this place. That's the trouble. I was afraid of this, but I thought you knew what you were about when you said you could stand it for a while."

"Oh, it isn't the house itself, Martin," she hastened to correct truthfully, sure that she had gone too far. "I - I - know we'll be happy."

Again this talk about happiness. He did not like it. He had never hunted for happiness, and he was contented. Why should she persist in this eternal search for this impossible condition? He supposed that occasionally children found themselves in it, but surely grown-ups could not expect it. The nearest they could approach it was in forgetting that there was such a state by finding solace in constant occupation.

"Let's eat," he announced. "I'm sick of this wrangling. Seems to me you're not starting off just right."

Rose hastened to prepare the meal, finding it more difficult to be cheerful as she realized how indifferent Martin was to her feelings, if only she presented a smooth surface. He had not seemed even to notice how orderly and freshened everything was. She thought of the new experience soon to be hers. Could it make up for all the understanding and friendly appreciation that she saw only too clearly would be missing in her daily life? Resolutely, she suppressed her doubts.

Martin, bothered by an odd feeling of strangeness in the midst of his own familiar surroundings, smoked his pipe in silence and studied Rose soberly. Why, he asked himself, was he unmoved by a woman who was so attractive? He liked the deftness with which her hands worked the pie dough, the quick way she moved between stove and table, yet mingled with this admiration was a slight but distinct hostility. How can one like and have an aversion to a person at the same time? he pondered. "I suppose," he concluded grimly, "it's because I'm supposed to love and adore her - to pretend a lot of extravagant feelings."

His mind travelled to the stock in the pasture. How stolid they were and how matter of fact and how sensible. They affected no high, nonsensical sentiments. Weren't they, after all, to be envied, rooted as they were in their solid simplicity? Why should human beings everlastingly try so hard to be different? He and Rose would have to get down to a genuine basis, and the quicker the better. Meanwhile he must remember that, whether he was glad or sorry, she was there, in his shack, because he had asked her to come.

As he ate his second helping of the excellent meal, he said pleasantly: "You do know how to cook, Rose."

Her soft gray-blue eyes brightened. "I love to do it," she answered quickly. "You must tell me the things you like best, Martin. If I had a real stove with a good oven, I could do much
better."

"Could you? We'll get one tomorrow."

"That'll be fine!" she smiled, eager to have all serene between them, and as she passed him to get some coffee her hand touched his in a swift caress. Instantly, Martin's cordiality vanished; his hostility toward her surged. Even as a boy he had hated to be "fussed over." Well, he had married and he would go through with it. If only Rose would be more matter of fact; not look at him with that expression which made him think of a confiding child. What business had a grown woman with such trust in her eyes, anyway?

It was quite gone, in the early dawn, as Rose sat on the edge of the bed looking at her husband. Never had she felt so far from him, so certain that he did not love her, as when she had lain quivering but impassive in his arms. "I might be just any woman," she had told herself, astounded and stricken to find how little she was touched by this experience which she had always believed bound heart to heart and crowned the sweet transfusion of affection from soul into soul. "It doesn't make any more difference to him who I am than who cooks for him."

Not that Martin had been unkind, except negatively. Intuitively, Rose understood that their first evening and night foreshadowed their whole lives. Not in what Martin would do, but in what he would not do, would lie her heartaches. Yet in her sad reflections there was no bitterness toward him; he had disappointed her, but perhaps it was only because she had taught herself to expect something rare, even spiritual, from marriage. Her idealism had played her a trick.

With the quiet relinquishment of this long-cherished dream, eagerness for the realization of an even more precious one took possession of her. She comforted herself with the thought that maybe life had brought Martin merely as a door to the citadel which looms, sparkling with dancing sunlight, in the midst of mysterious shadows. Motherhood - she would feel as if she were in another world. Out of all this disappointment would come her ultimate happiness.

Always struggling toward happiness, she was cheered too as the foundation for the house progressed. Everything would be so different, she told herself, once they were in their pretty new home. It was true she had given up a concrete floor for her cellar, but she had seen at once the good sense of having the concrete in the barn instead. Martin was right. While it would have been nice in the house, of course, it would not have begun to be the constant blessing to herself that it would now be to him. How much easier it would make keeping the barn clean! Why, it was almost a duty in a dairy barn to have such a floor and really she, herself, could manage almost as well with the dirt bottom. But when Martin began to discuss eliminating the whole upper story of the house, Rose protested.

"You won't use it," he had returned reasonably. "I'll keep my word, but when a body gets to figuring and sees all that can be built with that same money, it seems mighty foolish to put it into something that you don't really need."

As Martin looked at her questioningly, Rose felt suddenly unable to muster an argument for the additional sleeping-rooms. It was true that they were not actually necessary for their comfort; but the house as it had been decided upon was so interwoven with memories of her courtship and all that was lovable in Martin; it had become so real to her, that it was as if some dear possession were being torn to pieces before her eyes.

"I don't know why, Martin," she had answered, with a choky little laugh, "but it seems as if I just can't bear to give it up."

"Why?"

"I - I - like it all so well the way you planned it."

"Just liking a thing isn't always good reason for having it. It'll make lots more for you to take care of. What would you say if I was to prove to you that it would build a fine chicken-house, one for the herd boar, a concrete tank down in the pasture that'd save the cows enough trips to the barn to make 'em give a heap sight more milk, a cooling house for it and a good tool room?" Rose's eyes opened wide. "I can prove it to you."

That was all. But the shack filled with his disapproval of her reluctance to free him from his promise. She remembered one time when she had come home from school in a pelting rain that had changed, suddenly, to hail. There had seemed no escape from the hard, little balls and their cruel bruises. Just so, it seemed to her, from Martin, outwardly so calm as he read his paper, the harsh, determined thoughts beat thick and fast. Turn what way she would, they surrounded, enveloped and pounded down upon her. Her resolution weakened. Wasn't she paying too big a price for what was, after all, only material? The one time she and Martin had seemed quite close had been the moment in which she had agreed so quickly to change the location of the concrete floor. Now she had utterly lost him. She could scarcely endure the aloofness with which he had withdrawn into himself.

"Martin," she said a bit huskily, two evenings later, at supper, "I've decided that you are right. It is foolish and extravagant of me to want a second story when there are just the two of us. It will be better to have all those other things you told me about."

Martin did not respond; simply continued eating without looking up. This was a habit of his that nearly drove Rose desperate. In her father's household meals had always been friendly, sociable affairs. Patrick Conroy had been loquacious and by way of a wit; sharpened on his, Rose's own had developed. They had dealt in delicious nonsense, these two, and had her husband been of a different temperament she might have found it a refuge in her life with him. But, somehow, from the first, even before they were married, when with Martin, such chatter had died unuttered on Rose's tongue. The few remarks which she did venture, nowadays, had the effect of a disconcerting splash before they sank into the gloomy depths of the thick silence. Occasionally, in sheer self defense, she carried on a light monologue, but Martin's lack of interest gave her such an odd, lonely, stage-struck sensation that she, too, became untalkative, keeping to herself the ideas which chased through her ever-active mind. Innately just, she attributed this peculiarity of his to the fact that he had lived so long alone, and while it fretted her, she usually forgave him. But tonight, as no answer came, it seemed to her that if Martin did not at least raise his eyes, she must scream or throw something.

"It would be a godsend to be the sort who permits oneself to do such things," she told herself, a suggestion of a smile touching her lips, and mentally she sent dish after dish at him, watching them fall shattered to the floor. Dismay at the relief this gave her brought the dimples into her cheeks. Her voice was pleasant as she asked: "Martin, did you hear your spouse just now?"

Annoyance flitted across his face and crept into his tone as he answered tersely: "Of course, I heard you." Presently he finished his meal, pushed back his chair and went out.

Nothing further was said between them on the subject, but when the scaffolding went up she saw that it was for only one story. It might have comforted her a little, had she known what uneasy moments Martin was having. In spite of himself, he could not shake off the consciousness that he had broken his word. That was something which, heretofore, he had never done. But, heretofore, his promises had been of a strictly business nature. He would deliver so many bushels of wheat at such and such a time; he would lend such and such a piece of machinery; he would supply so many men and so many teams at a neighbor's threshing; he would pay so much per pound for hogs; he would guarantee so many eggs out of a setting or so many pounds of butter in so many months from a cow he was selling. A few such guarantees made good at a loss to himself, a few such loads delivered in adverse weather, a few such pledges of help kept when he was obliged actually to hire men, had established for him an enviable reputation, which Martin was of no mind to lose. Had Rose not released him from his promise he would have kept it. Even now he was disturbed as to what Fletcher and Fallon might think. But already he had lived long enough with his wife to understand something of the quality of her pride. Once having agreed to the change, she would carry it off with a dash.

Had Rose stood her ground on this matter, undoubtedly all her after life might have been different, but she was of those women whose charm and whose folly lie in their sensitiveness to the moods and contentment of the people most closely associated with them. They can rise above their own discomfort or depression, but they are utterly unable to disregard that of those near them. This gave Martin, who by temperament and habit considered only his own feelings, an incalculable advantage. His was the old supremacy of the selfish over the self sacrificing, the hard over the tender, the mental over the emotional. Add to this, the fact that with all his faults, perhaps largely because of them, perhaps chiefly because she cooked, washed, ironed, mended, and baked for him, kept his home and planned so continually for his pleasure, Martin was dear to Rose, and it is not difficult to understand how unequal the contest in which she was matched when her wishes clashed with her husband's. It was predestined that he, invariably, should win out.

Rose told her friends she and her husband had decided that the second story would make her too much work, and Martin noticed with surprise how easily her convincing statement was accepted. He decided, for his own peace of mind, that he had nothing with which to reproach himself. He had put it up to her and she had agreed. This principal concession obtained, other smaller ones followed logically and rapidly. The running water and bath in the house were given up for piping to the barn, and stanchions - then novelties in southeastern Kansas. The money for the hardwood floors went into lightning rods. Built-in cupboards were dismissed as luxuries, and the saving paid for an implement shed which delighted Martin, who had figured how much expensive machinery would be saved from rust. When it came to papering the walls he decided that the white plaster was attractive enough and could serve for years. Instead, he bought a patented litter-carrier that made the job of removing manure from the barn an easy task. The porches purchased everything from a brace and bit to a lathe for the new tool-room and put the finishing touches to the dairy. The result was a four-room house that was the old one born again, and such well-equipped farm buildings that they were the pride of the township.

Rose, who had surrendered long since, let the promises go to naught without much protest. Martin was so quietly domineering, so stubbornly persistent - and always so plausible - oh, so plausible! - that there was no resisting him. Only when it came to the fireplace did she make a last stand. She felt that it would be such a friendly spirit in the house. She pictured Martin and herself sitting beside it in the winter evenings.

"A house without one is like a place without flowers," she explained to him.

"It's a mighty dirty business," he answered tersely. "You would have to track the coal through the rest of the house and you'd have all those extra ashes to clean out."

"But you would never see any of the dirt," she argued with more than her usual courage, "and if I wouldn't mind the ashes I don't see why you should."

"We can't afford it."

"Martin, I've given in to you on everything else," she asserted firmly. "I'm not going to give this up. I'll pay for it out of my own money."

"What do you mean 'out of my own money'?" he asked sternly. "I told Osborne we'd run one account. If what is mine is going to be yours, what is yours is going to be mine. I'd think your own sense of fairness would tell you that."

As a matter of fact, Martin had no intention of ever touching Rose's little capital, but he had made up his mind to direct the spending of its income. He would keep her from putting it into just such foolishnesses as this fireplace. But Rose, listening, saw the last of her independence going. She felt tricked, outraged. During the years she had been at the head of her father's household, she had regulated the family budget and, no matter how small it had happened to be, she always had contrived to have a surplus. This notion of Martin's that he, and he alone, should decide upon expenditures was ridiculous. She told him so and in spite of himself, he was impressed.

"All right," he said calmly. "You can do all the buying for the house. Write a check with my name and sign your own initials. Get what you think we need. But there isn't going to be any fireplace. You can just set that down."

Voice, eyes, the line of his chin, all told Rose that he would not yield. Nothing could be gained from a quarrel except deeper ill feeling. With a supreme effort of will she obeyed the dictates of common sense and ended the argument abruptly.

But, for months after she was settled in the new little house, her eye never fell on the space where the fireplace should have been without a bitter feeling of revolt sweeping over her. She never carried a heavy bucket in from the pump without thinking cynically of Martin's promises of running water. As she swept the dust out of her front and back doors to narrow steps, she remembered the spacious porches that were to have been; and as she wiped the floors she had painted herself, and polished her pine furniture, she was taunted by memories of the smooth boards and the golden oak to which she had once looked forward so happily. This resentment was seldom expressed, but its flame scorched her soul.

Her work increased steadily. She did not object to this; it kept her from thinking and brooding; it helped her to forget all that might have been, all that was. She milked half the cows, separated the cream, took charge of the dairy house and washed all the cans. Three times a week she churned, and her butter became locally famous. She took over completely both the chickens and the garden. Often, because her feet ached from being on them such long hours, she worked barefoot in the soft dirt. According to the season, she canned vegetables, preserved fruit, rendered lard and put down pork. When she sat at meals now, like Martin she was too tired for conversation. From the time she arose in the morning until she dropped off to sleep at night, her thoughts, like his, were chiefly of immediate duties to be performed. One concept dominated their household - work. It seemed to offer the only way out of life's perplexities.

IV

ROSE-BUD IN THE DUST

UNDER this rigid regime Martin's prosperity increased. Although he would not have admitted it, Rose's good cooking and the sweet, fresh cleanliness with which he was surrounded had their effect, giving him a new sense of physical well-being, making his mind more alert. Always, he had been a hard worker, but now he began for the first time to take an interest in the scientific aspects of farming. He subscribed for farm journals and put real thought into all he did, with results that were gratifying. He grew the finest crop of wheat for miles around; in the season which brought others a yield of fifteen or twenty bushels to the acre, Martin averaged thirty-three, without buying a ton of commercial fertilizer. His corn was higher than anybody's else; the ears longer, the stalks juicier, because of his careful, intelligent cultivating. In the driest season, it resisted the hot winds; this, he explained, was the result of his knowing how to prepare his seed bed and when to plant - moisture could be retained if the soil was handled scientifically. He bought the spoiled acreage of his neighbors, which he cut up for the silo - as yet the only one in the county - adding water to help fermentation. His imported hogs seemed to justify the prices he paid for them, growing faster and rounder and fatter than any in the surrounding county. The chinch bugs might bother everyone else, but Martin seemed to be able to guard against them with fair success. He took correspondence courses in soils and fertilizers, animal husbandry and every related subject; kept a steady stream of letters flowing to and from both Washington and the State Agricultural College.

Now and then it crossed his mind that with the farm developing into such an institution it would be more than desirable to pass it on to one of his own blood, and secretly he was pleased when Rose told him a baby was coming. A child, a son, might bring with him a little of what was missing in his marriage with her. She irritated him more and more, not by what she did but by what she was. Her whole temperament, in so much as he permitted himself to be aware of it, her whole nature, jarred on his.

"When is it due?"

"October."

"It's lucky harvest will be over; silo filling, too," was his only comment.

In spite of Rose's three long years with Martin his lack of enthusiasm was like a sharp stab. What had she expected, she asked herself sternly. To be taken in his arms and rejoiced over as others were at such a moment? What did he care so long as he wouldn't have to hire extra help for her in the busy season! It was incredible - his hardness.

Why couldn't she hate him? He was mean enough to her, surely. "I'm as foolish as old Rover," she thought bitterly. The faithful dog lived for his master and yet Rose could not remember ever having seen Martin give him a pat. "When I once hold my own little baby in my arms, I won't care like this. I'll have someone else to fill my heart," she consoled herself, thrilling anew with the conviction that then she would be more than recompensed for everything. The love she had missed, the house that had been stolen from her - what were they in comparison to this growing bit of life? Meanwhile, she longed as never before to feel near to Martin. She could not help recalling how gallantly her father had watched over her mother when she carried her last child and how eagerly they all had waited upon her. At times, the contrast was scarcely to be borne.

Rose was troubled with nausea, but Martin pooh-poohed, as childish, the notion of dropping some of her responsibilities. Didn't his mares work almost to the day of foaling? It was good for them, keeping them in shape. And the cows - didn't they go about placidly until within a few hours of bringing their calves? Even the sows - did they droop as they neared farrowing? Why should a woman be so different? Her child would be healthier and she able to bring it into the world with less discomfort to herself if she went about her ordinary duties in her usual way. Thus Martin, impersonally, logically.

"That would be true," Rose agreed, "if the work weren't so heavy and if I were younger."

"It's the work you're used to doing all the time, isn't it? Because you aren't young is all the more reason you need the exercise. You're not going to hire extra help, so you might just as well get any to-do out of your mind," he retorted, the dreaded note in his voice.

She considered leaving him. If she had earned her living before, she could again. More than once she had thought of doing this, but always the hope of a child had shone like a tiny bright star through the midnight of her trials. Since she had endured so much, why not endure a little longer and reap a dear reward? Then, too, she could never quite bring herself to face the pictures her imagination conjured of Martin, struggling along uncared for. Now, as her heart hardened against him, an inner voice whispered that everyone had a right to a father as well as a mother, and Martin might be greatly softened by daily contact with a little son or daughter. In fairness, she must wait.

Yet, she knew these were not her real reasons. They lay far deeper, in the very warp and woof of her nature. She did not leave Martin because she could not. She was incapable of making drastic changes, of tearing herself from anyone to whom she was tied by habit and affection - no matter how bitterly the mood of the moment might demand it. Always she would be bound by circumstances. True, however hard and adverse they might prove, she could adapt herself to them with rare patience and dignity, but never would she be able to compel them to her will, rise superbly above them, toss them aside. Her life had been, and would be, shaped largely by others. Her mother's death, the particular enterprise in which her father's little capital had been invested, Martin's peculiar temperament - these had moulded and were moulding Rose Wade. At the time she came to Martin's shack, she was potentially any one of a half dozen women. It was inevitable that the particular one into which she would evolve should be determined by the type of man she might happen to marry, inevitable that she would become, to a large degree, what he wished and expected, that her thoughts would take on the complexion of his. Lacking in strength of character? In power of resistance, certainly. Time out of mind, such malleability has been the cross of the Magdalenes. Yet in what else lies the secret of the harmony achieved by successful wives?

And as, her nausea passing, Rose began to feel a glorious sensation of vigor, she decided that perhaps, after all, Martin had been right. Child-bearing was a natural function. People probably made far too much fuss about it. Nellie came to help her cook for the threshers and, for the rest, she managed very well, even milking her usual eight cows and carrying her share of the foaming buckets.

All might have gone smoothly if only she had not overslept one morning in late September. When she reached the barn, Martin was irritable. She did not answer him but sat down quietly by her first cow, a fine-blooded animal which soon showed signs of restlessness under her tense hands.

"There! There! So Bossy," soothed Rose gently.

"You never will learn how to manage good stock," Martin criticized bitingly.

"Nor you how to treat a wife."

"Oh, shut up."

"Don't talk to me that way."

As she started to rise, a kick from the cow caught her square on the stomach with such force that it sent her staggering backward, still clutching the handle of the pail from which a snowy stream cascaded.

"Now what have you done?" demanded Martin sternly. "Haven't I warned you time and again that milk cows are sensitive, nervous? Fidgety people drive them crazy. Why can't you behave simply and directly with them! Why is it I always get more milk from mine! It's your own fault this happened - fussing around, taking out your ill temper at me on her. Shouting at me. What could you expect?"

For the first time in their life together, Rose was frankly unnerved. It seemed to her that she would go mad. "You devil!" she burst out, wildly. "That's what you are, Martin Wade! You're not human. Your child may be lost and you talk about cows letting down more milk. Oh God! I didn't know there was any one living who could be so cruel, so cold, so diabolical. You'll be punished for this some day - you will - you will. You don't love me - never did, oh, don't I know it. But some time you will love some one. Then you'll understand what it is to be treated like this when your whole soul is in need of tenderness. You'll see then what - "

"Oh, shut up," growled Martin, somewhat abashed by the violence of her broken words and gasping sobs. "You're hysterical. You're doing yourself as much harm right now as that kick did you."

"Oh, Martin, please be kind," pleaded Rose more quietly. "Please! It's your baby as much as mine. Be just half as kind as you are to these cows."

"They have more sense," he retorted angrily. And when Rose woke him, the following night, to go for the doctor, his quick exclamation was: "So now you've done it, have you?"

As the sound of his horse's hoofs died away, it seemed to her that he had taken the very heart out of her courage. She thought with anguished envy of the women whose husbands loved them, for whom the heights and depths of this ordeal were as real as for their wives. It seemed to her that even the severest of pain could be wholly bearable if, in the midst of it, one felt cherished. Well, she would go through it alone as she had gone through everything else since their marriage. She would try to forget Martin. She WOULD forget him. She must. She would keep her mind fixed on the deep joy so soon to be hers. Had she not chosen to suffer of her own free will, because the little creature that could be won only through it was worth so much more than anything else the world had to offer? She imagined the baby already arrived and visualized him as she hoped her child might be at two years. Suppose he were in a burning house, would she have the courage to rescue him? What would be the limit of her endurance in the flames? She laughed to herself at the absurdity of the question. How well she knew its answer! She wished with passionate intensity that she could look into the magic depths of some fairy mirror and see, for just the flash of one instant, exactly how her boy or girl really would look. How much easier that would make it to hold fast to the consciousness that she was not merely in pain, but was laboring to bring forth a warm flesh-and-blood child. There was the rub - in spite of her eagerness, the little one, so priceless, wasn't as yet quite definite, real. She recalled the rosy-checked, curly-haired youngster her fancy had created a moment ago. She would cling to that picture; yes, even if her pain mounted to agony, it should be of the body only; she would not let it get into her mind, not into her soul, not into the welcoming mother-heart of her.

Meanwhile, as she armored her spirit, she built a fire, put on water to heat, attended capably to innumerable details. Rose was a woman of sound experience. She had been with others at such times. It held no goblin terrors for her. Had it not been for Martin's heartlessness, she would have felt wholly equal to the occasion. As it was, she made little commotion. Dr. Bradley, gentle and direct, had been the Conroys' family physician for years. Nellie, who arrived in an hour, had been through the experience often herself, and was friendly and helpful.

She liked Rose, admired her tremendously and the thought - an odd one for Nellie - crossed her mind that tonight she was downright beautiful. When at dawn, Dr. Bradley whispered: "She has been so brave, Mrs. Mall, I can't bear to tell her the child is not alive. Wouldn't it be better for you to do so?" She shrank from the task. "I can't; I simply can't," she protested, honest tears pouring down her thin face.

"Could you, Mr. Wade?"

Martin strode into Rose's room, all his own disappointment adding bitterness to his words: "Well, I knew you'd done it and you have. It's a fine boy, but he came dead."

Out of the dreariness and the toil, out of the hope, the suffering and the high courage had come - nothing. As Rose lay, the little still form clasped against her, she was too broken for tears. Life had played her another trick. Indignation toward Martin gathered volume with her returning strength.

"You don't deserve a child," she told him bitterly. "You might treat him when he grew up as you treat me."

"I've never laid hand to you," said Martin gruffly, certain stinging words of Nellie's still smarting. When she chose, his sister's tongue could be waspish. She had tormented him with it all the way to her home. He had been goaded into flaring back and both had been thoroughly angry when they separated, yet he was conscious that he came nearer a feeling of affection for her than for any living person. Well, not affection, precisely, he corrected. It was rather that he relished, with a quizzical amusement, the completeness of their mutual comprehension. She was growing to be more like their mother, too. Decidedly, this was the type of woman he should have married, not someone soft and eager and full of silly sentiment like Rose. Why didn't she hold her own as Nellie did? Have more snap and stamina? It was exasperating - the way she frequently made him feel as if he actually were trampling on something defenseless.

He now frankly hated her. There was not dislike merely; there was acute antipathy. He took a delight in having her work harder and harder. It used to be "Rose," but now it was always "say" or "you" or "hey." Once she asked cynically if he had ever heard of a "Rose of Sharon" to which he maliciously replied: "She turned out to be a Rag-weed."

Yet such a leveller of emotions and an adjuster of disparate dispositions is Time that when they rounded their fourth year, Martin viewed his life, with a few reservations, as fairly satisfactory. He turned the matter over judicially in his mind and concluded that even though he cared not a jot for Rose, at least he could think of no other woman who could carry a larger share of the drudgery in their dusty lives, help save more and, on the whole, bother him less. He, like his rag-weed, had settled down to an apathetic jog.

Rose was convinced that Martin would make too unkind a father; he had no wish for another taste of the general confusion and disorganized routine her confinement had entailed. Besides, it would be inconvenient if she were to die, as Dr. Bradley quite solemnly had warned him she might only too probably. Without any exchange of words, it was settled there should not be another child - settled, he dismissed it. In a way, he had come to appreciate Rose, but it was absurd to compliment anyone, let alone a wife whom he saw constantly. Physically, she did not interest him; in fact, the whole business bored him. It was tiresome and got one nowhere. He decided this state of mind must be rather general among married people, and reasoned his way to the conclusion that marriage was a good thing in that it drove out passion and placed human animals on a more practicable foundation. If there had been the likelihood of children, he undoubtedly would have sought her from time to time, but with that hope out of their lives the attraction died completely.

When he was through with his work, it was late and he was sleepy. When he woke early in the morning, he had to hurry to his stock. So that which always had been less than secondary, now became completely quiescent, and he was satisfied that it should. It never occurred to him to consider what Rose might be thinking and feeling. She wondered about it, and would have liked to ask advice from someone - the older Mrs. Mall or Dr. Bradley - but habitual reserve held her back. After all, she decided finally, what did it matter? Meanwhile, financially, things were going better than ever.

Martin had the most improved farm in the neighborhood; he was looked up to by everyone as one of the most intelligent men in the county, and his earnings were swelling, going into better stock and the surplus into mortgages which he accumulated with surprising rapidity. Occasionally, he would wonder why he was working so hard, saving so assiduously and investing so consistently. His growing fortune seemed to mean little now that his affluence was thoroughly established. For whom was he working? he would ask himself. For the life of him, he could not answer. Surely not for his Rag-weed of Sharon. Nellie? She was well enough fixed and he didn't care a shot for her husband. Then why? Sometimes he pursued this chain of thought further, "I'll die and probably leave five times as much as I have now to her and who knows what she'll do with it? I'll never enjoy any of it myself. I'm not such a fool as to expect it. What difference can a few thousand dollars more or less make to me from now on? Then why do I scheme and slave? Pshaw! I've known the answer ever since I first turned the soil of this farm. The man who thinks about things knows there's nothing to life. It's all a grinding chase for the day when someone will pat my cheek with a spade."

He might have escaped this materialism through the church, but to him it offered no inducements. He could find nothing spiritual in it. In his opinion, it was a very carnal institution conducted by very hypocritical men and women. He smiled at their Hell and despised their Heaven. Their religion, to him, seemed such a crudely selfish affair. They were always expecting something from God; always praying for petty favors - begging and whining for money, or good crops, or better health. Martin would have none of this nonsense. He was as selfish as they, probably more so, he conceded, but he hoped he would never reach the point of currying favor with anyone, even God. With his own good strength he would answer his own prayers. This farm was the nearest he would ever come to a paradise and on it he would be his own God. Rose did not share these feelings. She went to church each Sunday and read her Bible daily with a simple faith that defied derision. Once, when she was gone, Martin idly hunted out the Song of Solomon. His lips curled with contempt at the passionate rhapsody. He knew a thing or two, he allowed, about these wonderful Roses of Sharon and this Song of Songs. Lies, all lies, every word of it! Yet, in spite of himself, from time to time, he liked to reread it. He fancied this was because of the sardonic pleasure its superlative phrases gave him, but the truth was it held him. He despised sentiment, tenderness, and, by the strangeness of the human mind, he went, by way of paradox, to the tenderest, most sublime spot in a book supreme in tenderness and sublimity.

At forty, he owned and, with the aid of two hired hands, worked an entire section of land. The law said it was his and he had the might to back up the law. On these six hundred and forty broad acres he could have lived without the rest of the world. Here he was King. Other farms he regarded as foreign countries, their owners with impersonal suspicion. Yet he trusted them after a fashion, because he had learned from many and devious dealings with a large assortment of people that the average human being is honest, which is to say that he does not steal his neighbor's stock nor fail to pay his just debts if given plenty of time and the conditions have the explicitness of black and white. He knew them to be as mercenary as himself, with this only difference: Where he was frankly so, they pretended otherwise. They bothered him with their dinky deals, with their scrimping and scratching, and their sneaky attempts to hide their ugliness by the observance of one set day of sanctuary. Because they seemed to him so two-faced, so trifling, so cowardly, he liked to "stick" them every time he had a fair chance and could do it within the law. It was his favorite game. They worked so blindly and went on so stupidly, talking so foolishly, that it afforded him sport to come along and take the bacon away from them.

All held him a little in awe, for he was of a forbidding bearing, tall, grave and thoughtful; accurate in his facts and sure of himself; slow to express an opinion, but positive in his conclusions; seeking no favors, and giving none; careful not to offend, indifferent whether he pleased. He would deceive, but never insult. The women were afraid of him, because he never "jollied." He had no jokes or bright remarks for them. They were such useless creatures out of their particular duties. There was nothing to take up with them. Everyone rendered him much the same respectful manner that they kept on tap for the leading citizens of the town, David Robinson, for instance. Indeed, Martin himself was somewhat of a banker, for he was a stockholder and director of the First State Bank, where he was looked up to as a shrewd man who was too big even for the operation of his magnificent farm. He understood values. When it came to loans, his judgment on land and livestock was never disputed. If he wanted to make a purchase he did not go to several stores for prices. He knew, in the first place, what he should pay, and the business men, especially the hardware and implement dealers, were afraid of his knowledge, and still more of his influence.

About Rose, too, there was a poise, an atmosphere of background which inspired respect above her station. When

Mrs. Wade said anything, her statement was apt to settle the matter, for on those subjects which she discussed at all, she was an authority, and on those which she was not, her training in Martin's household had taught her to maintain a wise silence. The stern self-control had stolen something of the tenderness from her lips. There were other changes. The sunlight had faded from her hair; the once firm white neck was beginning to lose its resilience. Deep lines furrowed her cheeks from mouth to jaw, and fine wrinkles had slipped into her forehead. There were delicate webs of them about her patient eyes, under which lack of sleep and overwork had left their brown shadows. Since the birth of her baby she had become much heavier and though she was still neat, her dresses were always of dark colors and made up by herself of cheap materials. For, while she bought without consulting Martin, her privilege of discretion was confined within strict and narrow limits. He kept a meticulous eye on all her cancelled checks and knew to a penny what she spent. If he felt a respect for her thrift it was completely unacknowledged. They worked together with as little liking, as little hatred, as two oxen pulling a plow.

It had been a wise day for both, thought Fallon, when they had decided to marry - they were so well mated. What a model and enviable couple they were! To Rose it seemed the essence of irony that her life with Martin should be looked upon as a flower of matrimony. Yet, womanlike, she took an unconfessed comfort in the fact that this was so - that no one, unless it were Nellie, was sufficiently astute to fathom the truth. To be sure, the Wades were never spoken of as "happy." They were invariably alluded to as "good folks," "true blue," "solid people," "ideal husband and wife," or "salt of the earth."

Each year they gave a round sum to the church, and Martin took caustic gratification in the fact that, although his attitude toward it and religion was well known, he too was counted as one of the fold. To do its leaders justice, he admitted that this might have been partly through their hesitancy to hurt Rose who was always to be found in the thick of its sale-dinners, bazaars and sociables. How she was able to accomplish so much without neglecting her own heavy duties, which now included cooking, washing, mending and keeping in order the old shack for the hired men, was a topic upon which other women feasted with appreciative gusto, especially at missionary meetings when she was not present. It really was extraordinary how much she managed to put into a day. Early as Martin was up to feed his stock, she was up still earlier that she might lend a hand to a neighbor, harrowed by the fear that gathered fruit might perish. Late as he plowed, in the hot summer evenings, her sweaty fingers were busy still later with patching, brought home to boost along some young wife struggling with a teething baby. She seemed never too rushed to tuck in an extra baking for someone even more rushed than herself, or to make delicious broths and tasty dishes for sick folk. In her quiet way, she became a real power, always in demand, the first to be entrusted with sweet secrets, the first to be sent for in paralysing emergencies and moments of sorrow. The warmth of heart which Martin ridiculed and resented, intensified by its very repression, bubbled out to others in cheery helpfulness, and blessed her quick tears.

Of her deep yearning for love, she never spoke. Just when she would begin to feel almost self-sufficient it would quicken to a throbbing ache. Usually, at such times, she buried it determinedly under work. But one day, yielding to an impulse, she wrote to Norah asking if her little namesake could come for a month's visit.

"I know she is only seven," the letter ran, "but I am sure if she were put in care of the conductor she would come through safely, and I do so want to see her." After long hesitation, she enclosed a check to cover expenses. She was half frightened by her own daring and did not tell Martin until she had received the reply giving the date for the child's arrival.

"I earned that, Martin," she returned determinedly to his emphatic remonstrance. "And when the check comes in it's going to be honored."

"A Wade check is always honored," was his cryptic assertion. "I merely say," he added more calmly, "that if we are to board her, and I don't make any protest over that at all, it seems to me only fair that her father should have bought the ticket."

"Maybe you're right - in theory. But then she simply couldn't have come and I've never seen her. I first knew of her the very day you asked me to marry you. I've thought of her, often and often. Her mother named her after me and calls her 'Little Rose of Sharon, Illinois'."

"Another rag-weed, probably," said Martin, shortly. Yet, to his own surprise, he was not altogether sorry she was to come – this house of his had never had a child in it for more than a few hours. He was rather curious to find out how it would seem. If only her name were not Rose, and if only she were not coming from Sharon.

But little Rose, with her dark brown curls, merry expression, roguish nose and soft radiance swept all his misgivings and prejudices before her. One might as well hold grudges against a flower, he thought. He liked the confiding way she had of suddenly slipping her little hand into his great one. Her prattle amused him, and he was both flattered and worried by the fearlessness with which she followed him everywhere. She seemed to bring a veritable shower of song into this home of long silences. The very chaos made Mrs. Wade's heart beat tumultuously, and once when Martin came upon the little girl seated solemnly in the midst of a circle of corncob dolls, his throat contracted with an extraordinary tightness.

"You really are a rose - a lovely, sweet brown Rose of Sharon," he had exclaimed, forgetting his wife's presence and not stopping to think how strange the words must sound on his lips. "If you'll give me a kiss, I'll let you ride on old Jettie."

The child scrambled to her feet and, seated on his broad shoulder, granted the demand for toll. Her aunt's eyes filled. This was the first time she had ever heard Martin ask for something as sentimental as a kiss. She was thoroughly ashamed of herself for it - it was really too absurd! - but she felt jealousy, an emotion that had never bothered her since they had been married. And this bit of chattering femininity had caused it. Mrs. Wade worked faster.

The kiss was like the touch of silk against Martin's cheek. He felt inexplicably sad as he put the child down again among her playthings. There was, he realized with a shock, much that he was missing, things he was letting work supplant. He wished that boy of theirs could have lived. All might have been different. He had almost forgotten that disappointment, had never understood until this moment what a misfortune it had been, and here he was being gripped by a more poignant sense of loss than he had ever before felt, even when he had lost his mother.

Wonderful as little Rose was, she was not his own. But, he wondered suddenly, wasn't this aching sense of need perhaps something utterly different from unsatisfied paternal instinct? He turned his head toward the kitchen where his Rag-weed was working and asked himself if she were gone and some other woman were here - such as little Rose might be when she grew up, one to whom he went out spontaneously, would not his life be more complete and far more worth while? What a fool he was, to bother his head with such get-nowhere questions! He dismissed them roughly, but new processes of thought had been opened, new emotions awakened.

Meanwhile, little Rose's response to his clumsy tenderness taught him many unsuspected lessons. He never would have believed the pleasure there could be in simply watching a child's eyes light with glee over a five-cent bag of candy. It began to be a regular thing for him to bring one home from Fallon, each trip, and the gay hunts that followed as she searched for it - sometimes to find the treasure in Martin's hat, sometimes under the buggy seat, sometimes in a knobby hump under the table-cloth at her plate - more than once brought his rare smile. For years afterward, the memory of one evening lingered with him. He was resting in an old chair tipped back against the house, thinking deeply, when the little girl, tired from her play, climbed into his lap and, making a cozy nest for herself in the crook of his arm, fell asleep. He had finished planning out the work upon which he had been concentrating and had been about to take her into the house when he suddenly became aware of the child's loveliness. In the silvery moonlight all the fairy, flower-like quality of her was enhanced. Martin studied her closely, reverently. It was his first conscious worship of beauty. Leaning down to the rosy lips he listened to the almost imperceptible breathing; he touched the long, sweeping lashes resting on the smooth cheeks and lifted one of the curls the wind had been ruffling lightly against his face. With his whole soul, he marvelled at her softness and relaxation. A profound, pitying rebellion gripped him at the idea that anything so sweet, so perfect must pass slowly through the defacing furnaces of time and pain. "Little Rose of Sharon!" he thought gently, conscious of an actual tearing at his heart, even a startling stinging in his eyes. With an abruptness that almost awakened her, he carried her in to his wife.

Mrs. Wade felt an inexplicable hurt at the decidedness of little Rose's preference for Martin. She could not understand it. She took exquisite care of her, cooked the things she liked best, let her mess to her heart's content in the kitchen, made her dolls pretty frocks, cuddled her, told her stories and stopped her work to play with her on rainy days - but she could not win the same affection the little girl bestowed so lavishly on Martin. If left to herself she was always to be found with the big, silent man.

As the month's visit lengthened into three, it was astonishing what good times they had together. If he was pitching hay, her slender little figure, short dress a-flutter, was to be seen standing on the fragrant wagonload. At threshing time, she darted lightly all over the separator, Martin's watchful eye constantly upon her, and his protective hand near her. She went with him to haul the grain to mill and was fascinated by the big scales. On the way there and back he let her hold the great lines in her little fists. In the dewy mornings, she hop-skipped and jumped by his side into the pasture to bring in the cows. She flitted in and out among them during milking time.

"I think she makes them too nervous, Martin," Rose had once remarked. "Better run out, darling, until we finish and then come help auntie in the dairy."

"They might as well get used to her," he had answered tersely. "It'll hurt her feelings to be sent away."

Rose could scarcely believe her ears. Memories, bitter, intolerable, crowded upon her. Had the little girl really changed Martin so completely? Oh, if only her boy could have lived! Perhaps she had made a great mistake in being so determined not to have another. Was it too late now? She looked at her husband. Well as she knew every detail of his fine, clean cut features, his broad shoulders and rippling muscles, they gave her a sudden thrill. It was as if she were seeing him again for the first time in years. If only he could let a shadow of this new thoughtfulness and kindliness fall on her, they might even yet bring some joy into each other's lives. They had stepped off on the wrong foot. Why, they really hadn't been even acquainted. They had been led into thinking so because of the length of time they had both been familiar figures in the same community. Beyond a doubt, if they were being married today, and she understood him as she did now, she could make a success of their marriage. But, as it was, Martin was so fixed in the groove of his attitude of utter indifference toward her that she felt there was little chance of ever jogging him out of it. To Rose, the very fact that the possibility of happiness seemed so nearly within reach was what put the cruel edge to their present status.

She did not comprehend that Martin definitely did not want it changed. Conscious, at last, that he was slowly starving for a woman's love, beginning to brood because there was no beauty in his life, he was looking at her with eyes as newly appraising as her own. He remembered her as she had been that day in the bank, when he had thought her like a rose. She had been all white and gold then; now, hair, eyes, skin, and clothes seemed to him to be of one earthy color. Her clean, dull calico dress belted in by her checked apron revealed the ungraceful lines of her figure. She looked middle-aged and unshapely, when he wanted youth and an exquisite loveliness. Well, he told himself, harshly, he was not likely to get it. There was no sense in harboring such notions. They must be crushed. He would work harder, much harder, hard enough to forget them. There was but one thing worth while - his farm. He would develop it to its limits.

Accordingly, when little Rose returned to Sharon, he and his Rag-weed soon settled themselves to the old formula of endless toil, investing the profits in sound farm mortgages that were beginning to tax the capacity of his huge tin box in the vault of the First State Bank.

V

DUST BEGETS DUST

YET, through the Wades' busy days the echo of little Rose's visit lingered persistently. Each now anxiously wanted another child, but both were careful to keep this longing locked in their separate bosoms. Their constraint with each other was of far too long a standing to permit of any sudden exchange of confidences. It was with this hope half-acknowledged, however, and in her mind the recent memories of a more approachable Martin, that Rose began to make a greater effort with her appearance. By dint of the most skillful maneuvering, she contrived to purchase herself a silk dress - the first since her marriage. It was of dark blue crepe-de-chine, simply but becomingly made, the very richness of its folds shedding a new luster over her quiet graciousness and large proportions. Even her kind, capable hands seemed subtly ennobled as they emerged from the luscious, well fitting sleeves, and the high collar, with its narrow edge of lace, stressed the nobility of her fine head. When she came home from church, she did not, as she would have heretofore, change at once into calico, but protected by a spick and span white apron, kept on the best frock through dinner and, frequently, until chore time in the afternoon. In the winter, too, she was exposed less to sun and wind and her skin lost much of its weathered look. She took better care of it and was more careful with the arrangement of her hair. Gradually a new series of impressions began to register on Martin's brain.

One Sunday she came in fresh and ruddy from the drive home in the cold, crisp air. Martin found it rather pleasant to watch her brisk movements as she prepared the delayed meal. He observed, with something of a mental start, that today, at least, she still had more than a little of the old sumptuous, full-blown quality. It reminded him, together with the deft way in which she hurried, without haste, without flurry, of their first evening in the shack, nearly seven years ago. How tense they both had been, how afraid of each other, how she had irritated him! Well, he had grown accustomed to her at last, thanks be. Was he, perhaps, foolish not to get more out of their life - it was not improbable that a child might come. Why had he been taking it so for granted that this was out of the question? When one got right down to it, just what was the imaginary obstacle that was blocking the realization of this deep wish? Her chance of not pulling through? He'd get her a hired girl this time and let her have her own head about things. She'd made it all right once, why not again? The settledness of their habitual neutrality? What of it? He would ignore that. It wasn't as if he had to court her, make explanations. She was his wife. He didn't love her, never had, never would, but life was too short to be overly fastidious. It was flying, flying - in a few more years he would be fifty. Fifty! And what had it all been about, anyway? He did have this farm to show for his work - he had not made a bad job of that, he and his Rag-weed. In her own fashion she was a good sort, and better looking than most women past forty.

Rose felt the closeness of his scrutiny, sensed the unusual cordiality of his mood, but from the depths of her hardly won wisdom took no apparent notice of it. She knew well enough how not to annoy him. If only she had not learned too late! What was it about Martin, she wondered afresh, that had held her through all these deadening years? Her love for him was like a stream that, disappearing for long periods underground, seemed utterly lost, only to emerge again unexpectedly, cleared of all past murkiness, tranquil and deep.

This unspoken converging of minds, equivocal though it was

on Martin's part, resulted gradually in a more friendly period. Rose always liked to remember that winter, with its peace that quenched her thirsty heart and helped to blur the recollection of old unkindnesses long since forgiven, but still too vividly recalled. When, a year later, Billy was born, she was swept up to that dizzy crest of rapture which, to finely attuned souls, is the recompense and justification of all their valleys.

Martin watched her deep, almost painful delight, with a profound envy. He had looked forward, with more anticipation than even he himself had realized, to the thrill which he had supposed fatherhood would bring, taking it entirely for granted that he would feel a bond with this small reincarnation of his own being, but after the first week of attempting to get interested in the unresponsive bundle that was his son, he decided the idea of a baby had certainly signified in his mind emotions which this tiny, troublesome creature, with a voice like a small-sized foghorn, did not cause to materialize. No doubt when it grew into a child he would feel very differently toward it - more as he did toward little Rose, but that was a long time to wait, and meanwhile he could not shake off a feeling of acute disappointment, of defeated hopes.

By the end of the second month, he was sure he must have been out of his senses to bring such a nuisance upon himself and into his well-ordered house. Not only was his rest disturbed with trying regularity by night, and his meals served with an equally trying irregularity by day, but he was obliged to deal with an altogether changed wife. For, yielding as Rose was in all other matters, where Billy was concerned she was simply imperturbable. At times, as she held the chubby little fellow to her breast or caught and kissed a waving pink foot, she would feel a sense of physical weakness come over her - it seemed as if her breath would leave her. Martin could be what he might; life, at last, was worth its price. With the courage of her mother-love she could resist anything and everyone.

To her, the relative importance of the farm to Billy was as simple as a problem in addition. She had lost none of her old knack for turning off large amounts of work quickly, but she firmly stopped just short of the point where her milk might be impaired by her exertions. Martin had insisted that the requirement for hired help was over; however, in despair over his wife's determined sabotage, it was Martin himself who commanded that the girl be reinstated for another two months.

Rose was a methodical mother and not overly fussy. As soon as Billy could sit in a highchair or an ordinary packing box on the floor, she kept him with her while she went about her different tasks, cooing and laughing with him as she worked, but when he needed attention she could disregard calling dishes, chickens, half-churned butter, unfinished ironing, unmilked cows or an irate husband with a placidity that was worthy of the old Greek gods. Martin was dumbfounded to the point of stupefaction. He was too thoroughly self-centred, however, to let other than his own preferences long dominate his Ragweed's actions. Her first duty was clearly to administer to his comfort, and that was precisely what she would do. It was ridiculous, the amount of time she gave to that baby - out of all rhyme and reason. If she wasn't feeding him, she was changing him; if she wasn't bathing him she was rocking him to sleep. And there, at last, Martin found a tangible point of resistance, for he discovered from Nellie that not only was it not necessary to rock a baby, but that it was contrary to the new ideas currently endorsed. Reinforced, he argued the matter, adding that he could remember distinctly his own mother had never rocked Benny.

"Yes, and Benny died."

"It wasn't her fault if he did," he retorted, a trifle disconcerted.

"I don't know about that. She took chances I would never take with Billy. She sacrificed him, with her eyes open, for you and Nellie - gave him up so that you could have this farm."

Martin did not care for this new version. "What has that to do with the question?" he demanded coldly.

"Just this - your mother had her ideas and I have mine. I am going to raise Billy in my own way." But, for weeks thereafter she managed with an almost miraculous adroitness to have him asleep at meal times.

At seven months, Billy was the most adorable, smiling, cuddly baby imaginable, with dimples, four teeth and a tantalizing hint of curl in his soft, surprisingly thick, fawn-colored hair. Already, it was quite evident that he had his mother's sensitive, affectionate nature. If only his father had picked him up, occasionally, had talked to him now and then, he scarcely could have resisted the little fellow's crowing, sweet-tempered, responsive charm, but resentment at the annoyance of his presence was now excessive. For the present, Martin's only concern in his son consisted in seeing to it that his effacement was as nearly complete as possible.

The long-impending clash came one evening after a sultry, dusty day when Rose, occupied with a large washing in the morning and heavy work in the dairy in the afternoon, realized with compunction that never had she come so near to neglecting her boy. Tired and hot from fretting, he had been slow about going to sleep, and was just dozing off, when Martin came in, worn out and hungry.

"Isn't supper ready yet?"

"All but frying the sausage," Rose answered, achieving a pleasant tone in spite of her jadedness. "He's almost turning the corner - hear his little sleepy song? Sit down and cool off. I'll have it ready by the time you and the boys are washed."

Under its thick coat of tan, Martin's face went white. "I've had enough of this," he announced levelly. "You'll put him down and fry that meat."

"Wait just a minute," she coaxed; "he'll be off for the night and if you wake him, he'll cry and get all worked up."

"You heard what I said." His tone was vibrant with determination. "How am I going to keep hired men if you treat them like this? When they come in to eat, they want to find their food on the table."

"This doesn't often happen any more and they know, good and well, I make it up to them in other ways," returned Rose truthfully.

For answer, he crossed over to her quickly, reached down and took the baby from her.

"What are you going to do with him?" she demanded, a-tremble with rage and a sense of impotent helplessness, as, avoiding her quick movement, Martin went into the bedroom.

"Let him go to sleep as other children do, while you finish getting supper. Do you want to make a sissy of him?"

"A lot you care what he becomes!" she flashed, conflicting impulses contending for mastery, as Billy, now thoroughly awake and seeing his mother, began to cry, pleading to her with big blue eyes and out-stretched arms to take him. She started forward, but Martin stepped between herself and the crib.

"Martin Wade, let me pass. He's mine."

"It isn't going to hurt him to cry. He does it often enough."

"If you had a really cross baby around you'd know how good and reasonable Billy is," she flamed, torn by the little sobs.

"You get out to that kitchen," he ordered, more openly angry than Rose had ever seen him. "I've had enough of this talk, do you hear, and enough of this way of doing. Don't you set foot in here again till supper's over. I've had quite enough, too, of jumping up and down to wait on myself."

Confusedly, Rose thought of her countless hours of lost sleep, her even yet unrecovered strength, the enormous readjustment of her own life in her sincere efforts to do her best by the whole household, her joyous acceptance of all the perpetual self-denial her new duties to Billy necessitated. In comparison, the inconveniences to which Martin had been put seemed trifling. The occasional delays, and the unusual bother of stepping to the stove, now and then, to pour himself and the men a hot cup of coffee - this was their sum total. And how injured he really felt! The injustice of it left her speechless. Nails biting into her hands in her struggle for self-control, she left the room. With a slam of the door behind him, Martin followed her.

Blindly she strove for reason. Billy would simply cry himself to sleep - it was bad for his whole nervous system, but it would not actually make him sick. What a chaos must be in that little heart! His mother had failed him for the first time in his life. It was cruel, the way Martin had forced her to this, and as she listened, for the next half hour, to the muffled sound of Billy's crying and saw how impervious to it Martin was, she knew that never again could things be the same between her husband and herself.

But when, supper over, she found the corners of the rosebud mouth still pathetically down and Billy's breath still quivering in long gasps, she gathered the snuggly body to her and vowed in little broken love-words that from now on his father should have no further opportunities for discipline. Knowing him as she did, she should have trained the baby in the first place to go to sleep alone, should have denied herself those added sweet moments. After this she would be on her guard, forestall Martin, do tenderly what he would do harshly. Never again should her boy be made to suffer through any such mistaken selfishness of hers.

And though, after a while, the importance of this episode

Shrank to its true proportions, she never forgot or broke this promise. It would have been literally impossible for her to touch Billy, even when he was naughtiest and most exasperating, with other than infinite love, but she had an even firmness of her own. As sensitive as herself, adoring her to the point of worship, he was easily punished by her displeasure or five minutes of enforced quiet on a chair. The note of dread in her voice as she pleaded: "Hush, oh, hush, Billy, be good; quick, darling, papa's coming," was always effective. By ceaseless vigilance and indefatigable patience, she evaded further open rupture until the boy was three years old.

His shrieks had brought both his father and herself flying to the hog barn to find him dancing up and down as, frightened and aghast, he vainly attempted to beat off old Dorcas, a mammoth sow, from one of her day-old litter on which, having crushed it by accident, she was now quite deliberately feasting.

"God Almighty!" stormed Martin, hastily putting the little pigs back into the next pen. "Who let them in to her? That's her old trick."

"I opened the door," confessed Billy, troubled, frank eyes looking straight into his father's. "They were hungry; that one wanted her most." And, at the thought of the tragedy he had witnessed, he flung himself heartbroken into his mother's comforting arms.

"I'll whip you for this," said Martin sternly.

"Oh, please!" protested Rose, gathering the child closer. "Can't you see he's had a bitter enough lesson? His little heart is full."

"He's got to learn, once and for all, not to meddle with the stock. Come here."

"No! I won't have it. I'll see to it that he never does a thing like this again. He's too young to understand. He's never been struck in his life. You shan't."

Martin's cold blue eyes looked icily into his wife's blazing gray ones. "Don't act like a fool. Suppose he had gotten in there himself, and had fallen down - do you think she'd have waited to kill him? Where'd he be now - like that?" and he pointed to the half-eaten carcass.

Rose shuddered. There it was again - the same, familiar, disarming plausibility of Martin's, the old trick of making her seem to be the one in the wrong.

"I wish I had an acre for every good thrashing I got when I was a boy," he commented drily. "But in those days a father who demanded obedience wasn't considered a monster."

"If you only loved him, I wouldn't care," sobbed Rose. "I could stand it better to have you hit him in anger, but you're so hard, so cruel. You plan it all out so - how can you?"

Nevertheless, with a last convulsive hug and a broken "Mother can't help it, darling," she put Billy on his feet, her tormented heart wrung with bitterness as Martin took the clinging child from her and carried him away, hysterical and resisting.

"What else could I do?" she asked herself miserably, stabbed by the added fear that Billy might not forgive her. Could he understand how powerless she had been?

When once more the child was cuddled against her, she realized that in some mystical way there was a new bond between them, and as the days passed, she discovered it was not so much the whipping, but the unnatural perfidy of Dorcas that had scarred his mind. With his own eyes he had seen a mother devour her baby. He woke from dreams of it at night. Even the sight of her in the pasture contentedly suckling the remaining nine did not reassure him. The modern methods of psychology were then, to such women as Rose, a sealed book, but love and intuition taught her to apply them.

"You see, Billy," she explained, "hogs are meant to eat meat like dogs or bears or tigers. But they can live on just grain and grass, and that is what most farmers make them do because there is so much more of it and it costs so much less. Some of them feed what is called tankage. If old Dorcas could have had some of that she probably would not have eaten the little pig. You mustn't blame her too much, for she was just famishing for flesh, the way you are, sometimes, for a drink of water, when you've been playing hard." Thus rationalized, the old sow's conduct lost some of its grewsomeness, and in time, of course, the shock of the whole experience was submerged under other and newer impressions, but always the remembrance of it floated near the surface of his consciousness, his first outstanding memory of his father and the farm.

Inheriting a splendid physique from both parents, at six little Bill was as tall as the average child of eight, well set up and sturdy, afraid of nothing on the place except Martin, who, resenting his attitude, not unreasonably put the blame for it on his wife. "It's not what I do to him," he told her, "it's what you teach him to think I might do that makes him dislike me." To which Rose looked volumes, but made no reply.

Whatever the reason for the child's distrust, and honestly as he tried not to let it affect his feeling for his son, Martin found himself as much repelled by it as he had once been drawn to little Rose by her sweet faith and affection. Yet, in spite of the only too slightly veiled enmity between them, he was rather proud of the handsome lad and determined to give him a thorough stockman's and agriculturist's training. Some day he would run this farm, and Martin had put too much of his very blood into it not to make sure that the hands into which it would fall became competent. With almost impersonal approval he noticed the perfect co-ordination of the boy's muscles, his insatiable curiosity about machinery and his fondness for animals; all of which only made his pronounced distaste for work just that much more aggravating. He was, his father decided contemptuously, a dreamer.

Martin reached this conclusion early in his son's life - Bill was nine - and he determined to grind the objectionable tendency out of him. The youngster had a way of stopping for no reason whatever and just standing there. For all his iron self-control, it nearly drove the energetic man to violence. He would leave Bill in the barn to shovel the manure into the litter-carrier - a good fifteen-minute job; he would return in half an hour to find him sitting in the alleyway, staring down into his idle scoop.

"God Almighty!" Martin would explode. "How many times must I tell you to do a thing?"

The boy would look up slowly, like a frightened colt, expecting a blow, his non-resistance as angering as his indolence. Gazing at the enormous, imposing person who was his father, he would simply wait with wide open eyes - eyes that reminded Martin of a calf begging for a bucket of milk.

"I'm asking you! Answer when I speak. Have you lost the use of your tongue? What are you, anyway - a lump of jelly? Didn't I tell you to clean this barn? It's fly time and no wonder the cows suffer and slack up on their milk when there is a lazy bones like you around who won't even help haul away the manure."

"I was just a-goin' to."

"You should have been through long ago. What are you good for, is what I'd like to find out. You eat a big bellyful and what do you give in return? Do you expect to go through the world like this - having other people do your work for you? If this job isn't finished in fifteen minutes, I'll whip you."

Bill would work swiftly and painfully, for the carrier was high and hard for him to manipulate. But he would do his best, desperate over the threat, his whole nature rebelling, not so much at the task, as at the interruption of the pleasant stream of pictures which had been flowing so excitingly through his mind. Always it was like this - just when he was most blissfully happy, he was jerked back to some mean, dirty job by the stern, driving demands of his tireless father.

Without regard to the fact that harness is heavy, and a horse's back high, Martin would order him to hitch up. He was perfectly aware that it was too much for the child, but lack of affection, and a vague, extenuating belief that especially trying jobs developed one, made him merciless. The boy frequently boiled with rage, but he was so weaponless, so completely in his father's power - there was no escape from this tyranny. He knew he could not live without him; even his mother could not do that. His mother! What a sense of rest would come over him when he sat in her capacious lap, his head on her soft shoulder. With her cheek against his and her kind hand gently patting the back of his still chubby one, something hard in him always melted away.

"Why do I love you so, mama," he asked once, "and hate papa so?"

Mrs. Wade realized what was in his sore heart and hers ached for him, but she answered quietly: "You mustn't hate anybody, dear. You shouldn't."

"I don't hate anybody but him. I hate him and I'm afraid of him - just like you are."

"Oh, Billy," cried Rose, shocked to the quick. "You must never, never say I hate your father - when you're older you'll understand. He is a wonderful man."

"He's mean," said Billy succinctly. "When I get big I'm going to run away."

"From me? Oh, darling, don't think such thoughts. Papa doesn't intend to be mean. He just doesn't know what fun it is to play. You see, dear, when he was a boy like you, he had to work, oh, ever and ever so much more than you do - yes, he did," she nodded solemnly at Bill's incredulous stare. "And his mother never talked with him or held him close as I do you. She didn't have time. Aunt Nellie has told me all about it. He just worked and worked and worked - they all did. That's all there was in their life - just work. Why, when he was your age, his father was at war and papa and Grandmother Wade had to do everything. He did a man's share at fourteen and by the time he was fifteen, he ran this whole farm. Work has gotten to be a habit with him and it's made him different from a great many people. But he thinks that is why he's gone ahead and so he's trying to raise you the same way. If he really didn't care about you, Billy, it wouldn't bother him what you did."

In the silence that fell they could hear old Molly bellowing with pathetic monotony for her calf that had been taken from her. Yesterday she had been so proud, so happy. She had had such a hard time bringing it into the world, too. Martin had been obliged to tie a rope to its protruding legs and pull with all his strength. It didn't seem fair to think that the trusting-eyed little fellow had been snatched from her so soon, as if her pain had been an entirely negligible incident. Already, after six short weeks, he was hanging, drawn and quartered, in one of Fallon's meat-markets.

"I hate this place!" burst out the boy passionately. "I hate it!"

"All farms are cruel," agreed his mother quickly. "But I suppose they have to be. People must have milk and they must have veal."

At nine, though his fingers would become cramped and his wrists would' pain him, Bill had three cows to account for twice a day. At five in the morning, he would be shaken by Martin and told to hurry up. It would be dark when he stepped out into the chill air, and he would draw back with a shiver. Somewhere on these six hundred acres was the herd and it was his chore to find it and bring it in. He would go struggling through the pasture, unable to see twenty-five feet ahead of him, the cold dew or snow soaking through his overalls, his shoes becoming wet. Often he would go a mile north only to have to wander to another end of the farm before he located them. Other times, when he was lucky, they would be waiting within a hundred yards of the barn. Oh, how precious the warm bed was, and how his growing body craved a few more hours of sleep! He had a trick of pulling the sheet up over his head, as if thus he could shut out the world, but always his father was there to rout him out from this nest and set him none too gently on his feet; always there was a herd to be brought in and udders to be emptied. It made no difference to Martin that the daily walk to and from the district school was long, and left no spare time; it made no difference that the long hours at his lessons left the boy longing for play - always there was the herd, twice a day, cows and cows without end.

At twelve, Bill was plowing behind four heavy horses. He could run a mower, and clean a pasture of weeds in a day. He could cultivate and handle the manure spreader. In the hot, blazing sun, he could shock wheat behind Martin, who sat on the binder and cut the beautiful swaying gold. There wasn't a thing he could not do, but there was not one that he did with a willing heart. His dreams were all of escape from this grinding, harsh farm. It seemed to him that it was as ruthless as his father; that everything it demanded of him was, at best, just a little beyond his strength. If there was a lever to be pulled on the disk, very likely it was rusted and refused to give unless he yanked until he was short of breath and his heart beat fast; four horses were so unruly and hard to keep in place; the gates were all so heavy - they were not easy to lift and then drag open. It was such a bitter struggle every step of the way. It was so hard to plow as deeply as he was commanded. It was so wearing to make the seed bed smooth enough to measure up to his father's standard. Never was there a person who saw less to love about a farm than this son of Martin's. He even ceased to take any interest in the little colts.

"You used to be foolish about them," Martin taunted, "cried whenever I broke one."

"If I don't get to liking 'em, I don't care what happens to em,"

Bill answered with his father's own laconicism.

This chicken-heartedness, as he dubbed it, disgusted Martin, who consequently took a satisfaction in compelling the boy to assist him actively whenever there were cattle to be dehorned, wire rings to be pushed through bunches of pigs' snouts, calves to be delivered by force, young stuff to be castrated or butchering to be done. Often the sensitive lad's nerves were strained to the breaking point by the inhuman torture he was constantly forced to inflict upon creatures that had learned to trust him. There was a period when it seemed to him every hour brought new horrors; with each one, his determination strengthened to free himself as soon as possible from this life that was one round of toil and brutality.

Rose gave him all the sympathy and help her great heart knew. His rebellion had been her own, but she had allowed it to be ground out of her, with her soul now in complete surrender. And here was her boy going through it all over again, for himself, learning the dull religion of toil from one of its most fanatical priests. What if Bill, too, should finally have acquiescence to Martin rubbed into his very marrow, should absorb his father's point of view, grow up and run, with mechanical obedience, the farm he abhorred? The very possibility made her shudder. If only she could rescue him in some manner, help him to break free from this bondage. College - that would be the open avenue. Martin would insist upon an agricultural course, but she would use all her tact and rally all her powers that Billy might be given the opportunity to fit himself for some congenial occupation. Martin might even die, and if she were to have the farm to sell and the interest from the investments to live on, how happy she could be with this son of hers, so like her in temperament. She caught herself up sharply. Well, it was Martin himself who was driving her to such thoughts.

"You are like old Dorcas," she once told her husband, driven desperate by the exhausted, harrowed look that was becoming habitual in Bill's face. "You're trampling down your own flesh and blood, that's what you're doing - eating the heart out of your own boy."

"Go right on," retorted Martin, all his loneliness finding vent in his bitter sneer, "tell that to Bill. You've turned him against me from the day he was born. A fine chance I've ever had with my son!"

VI

DUST IN HIS EYES

SUCH was the relationship of the Wades when one morning the mail brought them a letter from Sharon, Illinois. Rose wrote that she was miserably unhappy with her step-mother. Could she live with them until she found a job? She had been to business college and was a dandy stenographer. Maybe Uncle Martin could help her get located in Fallon.

"Of course I will, if she's got her head set on working," was his comment. "I'll telegraph her to come right along. Might as well wire the fare, too, while I'm about it and tell her to let us know exactly when she can get here."

Mrs. Wade looked up quickly at this unusual generosity, yet she was, she realized, more startled than surprised. For had not little Rose been the one creature Martin had loved and to whom he had enjoyed giving pleasure? It had been charming - the response of the big, aloof man to the merry child of seven, but that child was now a woman, and, in all probability, a beautiful one. Wasn't there danger of far more complicated emotions which might prove even uprooting in their consequences? Mrs. Wade blushed. Really, she chided herself sternly, she wouldn't have believed she could be such an old goose - going out of her way to borrow trouble. If her husband was moved to be hospitable, she ought to be wholly glad, not petty enough to resent it. She would put such thoughts out of her mind, indeed she would, and welcome Rose as she would have wanted Norah to have welcomed Bill, had the circumstances been reversed. It would be lovely to have the girl about - she would be so much company, and the atmosphere of light-hearted youth which she would bring with her would be just what Billy needed. By the time Rose's answer came, saying she would arrive in two weeks, her aunt was genuinely enthusiastic.

"I wonder," said Martin, "if we could build on an extra room by then. If she's going to make this her home, she can't be crowded as if she was just here for a short visit. I'll hunt up Fletcher this afternoon."

Mrs. Wade's lips shut tight, as she grappled with an altogether new kind of jealousy. To think that Martin should delight in giving to an outsider a pleasure he had persistently denied his own son. How often had she pleaded: "It's a shame to make Billy sleep in the parlor! A boy ought to have one spot to himself where he can keep his own little treasures." But always she had been met with a plausible excuse or a direct refusal. "I suppose I ought to be thankful someone can strike an unselfish chord in him," she thought, wearily.

"You'll have to get some furniture," Martin continued placidly. "Mahogany's the thing nowadays."

"It's fearfully expensive," she murmured.

"Oh, I don't know. Might as well get something good while we're buying. And while you're at it, pick out some of those curtains that have flowers and birds on 'em and a pretty rug or two. I'll have Fletcher put down hard oak flooring; and I guess it won't make much more of a mess if we go ahead and connect up the house with the rest of the Delco system."

"It's about time," put in Bill, who had been listening round-eyed, until now actually more than half believing his father to be in cynical jest. "We're known all over the county as the place that has electric lights in the barns and lamps in the house."

"It hasn't been convenient to do it before," was the crisp answer.

Bill and his mother exchanged expressive glances. When was anything ever convenient for Martin Wade unless he were to derive a direct, personal satisfaction from it! Then it became a horse of quite another color. He could even become lavish; everything must be of the best; nothing else would do; no expense, as long as full value was received, was too great. Mrs. Wade found herself searching her memory. She was positive that not since those occasions upon which he had brought home the sacks of candy for the sheer sunshine of watching little Rose's glee had anyone's pleasure been of enough importance to him to become his own. All this present concern for her comfort talked far more plainly than words.

This time, Mrs. Wade admitted bravely to herself that her jealousy was not for Billy. It would have been far easier for her if she had known that Martin was thinking of their coming guest as he had last seen her thirteen years before. He realized, thoroughly, that she must have grown up, but before his mental eyes there still danced the roguish little girl he had held so tenderly in his arms and had so longed to protect and cherish.

He experienced a distinct sense of shock, therefore, when, tall, slender and smartly dressed, Rose stepped off the train and, throwing her arms impulsively around his neck, gave him an affectionate kiss. The feel of those soft, warm lips lingered strangely, setting his heart to pounding as he guided her down the platform.

"Uncle Martin, you haven't changed a bit!" she exclaimed joyously. "I was wondering if I'd recognise you - imagine! Somehow, I thought thirteen years would make a lot of difference, but you don't look a day older."

"You little blarney," he smiled, pleased nevertheless. "Well, here we are," and he stopped before his fine Cadillac.

"Oh, Uncle Martin," gasped Rose ecstatically. "What a perfectly gorgeous car! I thought all farmers were supposed to have Fords."

They laughed happily together.

"It's the best in these parts," he admitted complacently.

"It's too wonderful to think that it is really yours. Oh, Uncle Martin, do you suppose you could ever teach me to drive it?"

"It takes a good deal of strength to shift the gears, but you can have a try at it anyway, tomorrow."

"Oh-h-h!" she exulted, slipping naturally into their old comradeship.

Martin took her elbow as he helped her into the car. The firm young flesh felt good - it was hard to let go. His thumb and under finger had pressed the muscles slightly and they had moved under his touch. His hand trembled a bit. The grace with which she stepped up gave him another thrill. He was struck with her trim pump, and the several inches of silk stocking that flashed before his eyes, so unaccustomed to noticing dainty details, gave him a mingled sensation of delight and embarrassment. It had been many a day, many a year, since he had consciously observed his wife. She was too useful for him to permit himself to be influenced by questions of beauty into underrating her value, and he was a respectable husband, if not a kind one. They had jogged on so long together that he would have said he had ceased to be conscious of her appearance. But suddenly he felt that he could not continue to endure, for another day, the sight of the spreading, flat house-slippers which, because of her two hundred and forty pounds and frequently rheumatic feet, she wore about her work. Moreover, it was forcibly borne in upon him just what a source of irritation they had been. And they were only as a drop in the bucket! Well, such thoughts did no one any good. Thank heaven, from now on he would have Rose to look at.

They settled down beside each other in the front seat and he was aware that her lovely eyes, so violet-blue and ivory-white, were studying him admiringly. Here was a man, she was deciding, who for his age was the physical superior of any she had ever met. He was clearly one of those whom toil did not bend, and while, she concluded further, he might be taken for all of his fifty-four years it would be simply because of his austere manner.

Martin sustained her scrutiny until they were well out of Fallon and speeding along on a good level road. Then with a teasing "turn about's fair play," he, too, took a frank look, oddly stirred by the sophisticated touches which added so subtly to her natural beauty. From her soft, thick brown hair done up cleverly in the latest mode and her narrow eyebrows arched, oh, so carefully, and penciled with such skill, to that same trim provocative pump and disconcerting flash of silk-clad ankle, Rose had dash. Hers was that gift of style which is as unmistakable as the gift of song and which, like it, is sometimes to be found unexpectedly in any village or small town.

Martin drank in every detail wonderingly, with a kind of awe. All his life, it seemed to him, for the last thirteen years positively, he had known that somewhere there must be just such a woman whose radiance would set his heart beating with the rapture of this moment and whose moods would blend so easily with his own that she would seem like a very part of himself. And here she was, come true, sitting right beside him in his own car. For the first time in his whole life, Martin understood the meaning of the word happiness. It gripped and shook him and made his heart ache with a delicious pain.

"It's hard to believe," he murmured, "such a very small girl went away and such a very grown up little woman has come back. Let's see - twenty is it? My, you make me feel old - but you say I haven't changed much."

"You haven't. A little bit of gray, a number of tiny wrinkles about your eyes" - the tips of two dainty fingers touched them lightly - "and you're a bit thinner - that's all. Why you look so good to me, Uncle Martin, I could fall in love with you myself, if you weren't auntie's husband."

It was an innocent remark, and he understood it as such, but its effect on him was dynamic.

"You always were as pretty as a picture," he said slowly, his nerves tingling, "if a farmer's opinion is worth anything in that line."

This was twaddle, of course, and Martin knew it. Rather it was the city person's point of view he was inclined to belittle. He had the confidence in his superiority that comes from complete economic security and his pride of place was even more deeply rooted. Men of Martin's class who are able to gaze, in at least one direction, as far as eye can see over their own land, are shrewd, sharp, intelligent, and far better informed on current events and phases of thought than the people of commercial centers even imagine. There is nothing of the peasant about them. Martin knew quite well that dressed in his best clothes and put among a crowd of strange business men he would be taken for one of their own - so easy was his bearing, so naturally correct his speech.

Something of all this had already registered in Rose's mind. "Come on, Uncle Martin," she laughed, "flatter me. I just love it!"

"Very well, then, I'll say that you've come back as pretty a little woman as ever I've laid eyes on."

"Is that all? Oh, Uncle Martin, just pretty? The boys usually say I'm beautiful."

"You are beautiful - as beautiful as a rose. That's what you are, a red, red rose of Sharon - with your dove's eyes, your little white teeth like a flock of even sheep and your sweet, pretty lips like a thread of scarlet."

"Why, Uncle Martin!" exclaimed the girl, a trifle puzzled by the intensity of his quiet tone, and stressing their relationship ever so lightly. "You're almost a poet."

"You mean old King Solomon was," he retrieved himself quickly. "Don't you ever read the Bible?"

"I didn't know you did!"

"Oh, your old Uncle reads a little of everything," he returned with a reassuring commonplaceness of manner. He was thunderstruck at his outburst. Never had he had occasion to talk in that vein. He remembered how blunt he had been with the older Rose twenty years before - how he had jumped to the point at the start and landed safely; clinched his wooing, as he had since realized, by calling her his Rose of Sharon, and now he was saying the same thing over again, but, oh, how differently. If only he were thirty-four today, and unmarried!

"You always were the most wonderful person," beamed Rose, completely at her ease once more, "I used to simply adore you, and I'm beginning to adore you again."

"That's because you don't know what a glum old grouch I really am."

"You - a grouch? Oh, Uncle Martin!" Her merry, infectious laugh left no doubt of how ridiculous such a notion seemed.

"Oh, yes; I am."

"Nonsense. You'll have to prove it to me."

"Ask your aunt or Bill; they'll tell you." The acrimony in his tone did not escape her.

"Then they'll have to prove it to me," she corrected, her gaiety now a trifle forced. Aunt Rose never had appreciated him, was her quick thought. Even as a child she had sensed that.

"How are they?" she added quickly. "Bill must be a great boy by this time."

"Only a few inches shorter than I am," Martin answered indifferently. "He's one of the kind who get their growth early - by the time he's fifteen he'll be six feet."

"I'm crazy to see them."

"Well, there's your aunt now," he resumed drily as they drew up before the little house that contrasted so conspicuously with the fine brick silos and imposing barns. Gleaming with windows, they loomed out of the twilight, reminding one, in their slate-colored paint, of magnificent battleships.

The bright glare of the auto picked Mrs. Wade out for them as mercilessly as a searchlight. Where she had been stout thirteen years before, she was now frankly fat. Four keen eyes noted the soft, cushiony double chin, the heavy breasts, ample stomach, spreading hips, and thick shoulders, rounded from many years of bending over her kitchen table. Kansas wind, Kansas well-water and Kansas sun had played their usual havoc, giving her skin the dull sand color so common in the Sunflower State. She had come from her cooking and she was hot, beads of sweat trickling from the deep folds of her neck. Withal, there was something so comfortable and motherly about her, the kind, wise eyes behind the gold-rimmed glasses were so misty with welcome and unspoken thoughts of the dear mother Rose had lost, that the girl went out to her sincerely even as she marvelled that the same years on the same farm which had given one person added polish and had made him even more good looking than ever, could have changed another so completely and turned her into such a toil-scarred, frumpy, oldish woman. Why, when she had been talking with Uncle Martin he had seemed no older than herself - well, not quite that, of course, but she had just forgotten about his age altogether - until she saw Aunt Rose. No wonder whenever he spoke of his wife every intonation told how little he loved her. How could he care any more - that way?

Rose's first look of astonishment and her darting glance in his own direction were not lost on Martin. With an imperceptible smile, he accepted the unintended compliment, but he felt a pang when he noticed that to her Aunt went the same affectionate, impetuous embrace that she had given to him at the station.

"You're losing your head," he told himself sternly, driving into the garage, where, stopping his engine, he continued to sit motionless at the wheel. "That ought to be a lesson to you; she's just naturally warm-hearted and loving. Always was. You're no more to her than anybody else. Well, there's no fool like an old fool." Yet, deeper than his admitted thought was the positive conviction that already something was up between them. If not, why this excitement and wild happiness? To be sure, nothing had been said - really. It had all been so light. Rose was just a bit of a born flirt. But he, having laughed at love all his life, loved her deeply, desperately. Well, so much the worse for himself - it couldn't lead anywhere. Yet in spite of all his logic he knew that something was going to happen. Hang it all - just what? He was afraid to answer his own question; not because of any dread of what his wife might do - he was conscious only of a new, cold, impersonal hatred toward her because she stood between him and his Rose; nor was it qualms about his ability to win the girl's heart. Already, despite his inexperience with love technique, he was, in some mysterious manner, making progress. The community - his position in it? This was food for thought certainly, but it was not what worried him. Then why this feeling of dismay when he wanted to be only glad?

The question was still unanswered when he finally left the garage. With all his powers of introspection, he had not yet fathomed the fact that it was a fear of his own, until now utterly unsuspected, capacity for recklessness. Heretofore, he had been able to count on the certainty that his best judgment would govern all his actions. Now, he felt himself clutching, almost frantically, at the hard sense of proportion that never before had so much as threatened to desert him. He went about his chores in a grave, automatic way, absorbed in anything but agriculture. Hardly ever did he pass through his barn without paying homage to his own progressiveness and oozing approval of the mechanical milker, driven by his own electrical dynamo, the James Way stanchions with electric lights above, the individual drinking fountains at the head of each cow, the cork-brick floors, the scrupulously white-washed walls, and the absence of odor, with the one exception of sweet, fermented silage. But, tonight, he was not seeing these symbols of material superiority. Instead he was thinking of a girl with eyes as soft as a dove's, lips like a thread of scarlet and small white teeth as even as a flock of his own Shropshire sheep. What else did that old King Solomon say? God Almighty, he thought, there was a man who understood! He'd try to get a chance to reread that Song of Songs that was breaking his own heart with its joy and its sadness.

His reverie was broken abruptly by the jangling supper-bell. When he reached the back door Bill was already at the table and Rose, in a simple gown that brought out the appealing lines of her slim young body, was deftly helping his wife in the final dishing up. As Martin stood a moment, looking in at the bright scene and listening to the happy chatter, he heard her ask if he had got her a job. At sight of him she cried excitedly: "Oh, Uncle Martin! You can't think how I adore my beautiful room! And Bill says it was you who first thought of building it for me. You old darling! You and Aunt Rose are the best people in the whole wide world. How can I ever thank you?"

"I'll tell you," he smiled, "forget all about that job and just stay around here and make us all young. Time enough to work when you have to."

Mrs. Wade noticed how Bill's eyes widened at these words, so unlike his father, and soon she was acutely aware of her husband's marked agreeableness whenever he directed his conversation toward Rose. He even tried to include his son and herself in this new atmosphere, but with each remark in their direction his manner changed subtly. Toward herself, in particular, his feelings were too deep for him to succeed in belying them.

As the meal progressed, she realized that her dim forebodings were fast materializing into a certain danger. Unless she acted promptly this slip of a girl was going to affect, fundamentally, all their lives. Already, it seemed as though she had been amongst them a long time and had colored the future of them all. Mrs. Wade understood far better than her husband would have supposed that, in his own way, his married life had been as starved as her own; oh, far more so, for she had her boy. And while it was not at all likely, it was not wholly impossible that he might seek a readjustment. It seemed far-fetched for her to sit thus and feel that drama was entering their hard lives when nothing had really happened, but nevertheless - she knew. As, outwardly so calm, she speculated with tumbled thoughts on how it might end, she tried to analyze why it was that the prospect of a shake-up filled her with such a sense of disaster. Surely, it was not because of any reluctance to separate from Martin. Her life would be far easier if they went their own ways. With Bill, she could make a home anywhere, one that was far more real, in a house from which broken promises did not sound as from a trumpet. Ashes of resentment still smouldered against Martin because of that failure of his to play fair. She recalled the years during which she had helped him to earn with never an unexpected pleasure; reflected with bitterness that never, since they had cast their lives together, had he urged her to indulge in any sweet little extravagance, though he had denied himself nothing that he really wished. It was no riddle to her, as it had been to her niece earlier in the evening, why the same hard work had dealt so benignly with

Martin and so uncharitably with herself. She comprehended only too well that it was not that alone which had crushed her. It was his ceaseless domination over her, the utter subjugation of her will, her complete lack of freedom. She glanced across the table at him, astounded by his hearty laugh in response to one of Rose's sallies. It seemed incredible that it could be really Martin's. It had such a ring and came out so easily as if he were more inclined to merriment than to silence. Usually, he seemed made of long strips of thin steel, but under the inspiration of Rose's presence he had become animated, brisk, interesting. No wonder she was being drawn to him.

It was as if he had withheld from his wife a secret alchemy that had kept him handsome and attractive, as compelling as when he had come in search of herself so long ago. And now that the last vestige of her own bloom was gone, he was laughing at her, inwardly, as a cunning person does who plays a malicious trick on a simpler, more trusting, soul. Only it had taken twenty years to spring the point of this one. Hatred welled in her heart; a sad, weary hatred that knew no tears. She wished that she might hurt him as he had hurt her. Yet, with her usual honesty, she presently admitted how easy it would be for this malevolence to melt away - a word, a look, a gesture from Martin and the heart in her would flood with forgiveness; but the look did not come, the word was unuttered.

He was squandering, she continued to observe, sufficient evidence of his interest at the feet of this child who never would have missed it, while she, herself, who could have lifted mountains from her breast with one tenth of this appreciation, was left, as she always had been left, without the love her being craved, the love of a mate, rising full and strong to meet her own. It was a yearning that the most cherished of children could never satisfy and as she watched Martin and Rose her position seemed to her to be that of a hungry pauper, brought to the table of a rich gourmand, there to look on helplessly while the other toyed carelessly with the precious morsels of which she was in such extreme need. And what rankled was that these thoughts were futile, that too much water had run under the bridge, that it was her lot in Martin's life merely to accept what was offered her. She knew that the marks of her many hours of suppressed anguish, thousands of days of toil and long series of disappointments were thick upon her. She realized, too, how ironical it was that with all her work she should have grown to be so ungainly although Martin retained the old magnetism of his gorgeous physique. There was no doubt that if he chose, he could still hold a woman's devotion. Yes, for him there was an open road from this gray monotony, if he had the will and the courage to escape.

Suddenly, she found herself wondering what effect all this would have on Bill. She stole a surreptitious glance at him, but he, too, seemed to have been caught up by Rose's gay, good humor. Mrs. Wade sighed as she remembered how everyone had flocked around Norah. Rose had inherited her mother's charm. Such women were a race apart. They could no more be held responsible for trying to please than a flower for exhaling its fragrance. At what a lovely moment of life she was! Small wonder that Martin was captivated, but not even the shadow of harm must fall on that fresh young spirit while she was under their roof. If things went much further she would have it out with him. And this decision reached, Mrs. Wade felt her usual composure gradually return, nor did it again desert her during the long evening through which it seemed to her as if her husband must be some stranger.

VII

MARTIN BATTLES WITH DUST

THE human animal is a strange spectacle to behold, let alone comprehend. Not infrequently he goes along for years developing a state of mind, a consistent attitude, and then having got it thoroughly established does something in distinct contradiction to it. Martin had never cared for music, but when one evening, a little more than a week after Rose's arrival, she suggested, with a laughing lilt, her fondness for it, he agreed that he had missed it in his home and, to Bill's and Mrs. Wade's unbelieving surprise, dwelt at length upon his enjoyment of Fallon's band and his longing to blow a cornet. A little later, finding an excuse to leave, he drove into town on a mission so foreign to his iron-clad character that it seemed to cry against his every instinct, but which, for all that, he did with such simplicity as to indicate that it was the most natural step imaginable. He actually bought a two-hundred-dollar mahogany Victrola and an assortment of records, bringing both home with him in his car and, assisted eagerly by Bill, carrying them into the front room with an air that said it was a purchase he had been intending to make for a long time. Rose rewarded him with her bubbling delight and her aunt noticed with an odd constriction about her heart how Bill revelled at last in the new treasure, until now so hopelessly coveted. Martin had never shone to better advantage than this evening as he helped select and put on different pieces, lending himself to the mood of each. It was while a foot-stirring dance was on that Rose asked suddenly:

"Oh, Uncle Martin, do you know how?"

He shook his head. "You'll have to teach me to square up for learning to drive the car."

"That's a bargain; and I'll teach Bill too," she added with native tact. But Mrs. Wade, ill at ease in her own parlor, caught the afterthought quality of Rose's tone. There was no question but that it was for Martin she sparkled, sweet and spontaneous as she was. Decidedly, the time had come when definite action should not be delayed.

It was nearly twelve o'clock when they finally broke up and husband and wife found themselves alone in their own room. As they undressed, Mrs. Wade acted nervously, confused as to how to begin, while Martin whistled lightly and kept time by a slight bobbing of his head. She shot a meaning look in his direction.

"You seem happy, don't you?"

He stopped whistling instantly and assumed his more normal look of set sternness. This was the man she knew and she preferred him that way, rather than buoyant because of some other woman, even though that other was as lovable and innocent of any deliberate mischief as her niece. Not that she was jealous so much as she was hurt. When a woman has fortified herself, after years of the existence to which Mrs. Wade had submitted, with the final conviction that undoubtedly her husband's is a nature that cannot be other than it is, and then learns there are emotional potentialities not yet plumbed, not to mention a capacity for pleasant comradeship of which he has never vouchsafed her an inkling, she finds herself being ground between the millstones of an aching admission of her own deficiencies and a tattered, but rebellious, pride.

Martin, when her remark concerning his apparent happiness had registered, let his answer be a sober inspection of the garment he had just removed.

"I don't suppose you can talk to me now after such a strenuous evening," she went on more emphatically. And as he maintained his silence, she continued with: "Oh, don't think I'm blind, Martin Wade. I know exactly how far this has gone and I know how far it can go."

"What are you driving at?"

"You know perfectly well what I mean - the way you are behaving toward Rose."

"Are you trying to imply that I'm carrying on with her?"

"I certainly am. I'm not angry, Martin. I never was calmer than I am right now, and I don't intend to say things just for the sake of saying them. I only want you to know that I have eyes, and that I don't want to be made a fool of."

To her surprise, Martin came over to her and, looking at her steadily, returned with amazing candidness: "I'm not going to lie to you. You're perfectly welcome to know what's in my mind. I love her with every beat of my heart - she has brought something new into my life, something sacred - you've always thought I cared for nothing but work, that all I lived for was to plan and scheme how to make money. Haven't you? I don't blame you. It's what I've always believed, but tonight I've learned something." Mrs. Wade could see his blood quicken. "She has been in this house only a few days and already I am alive with a new fire. It seems as if these hours are the only ones in which I have ever really lived - nothing else matters. Nothing! If there could be the slightest chance of my winning her love, of making her feel as I am feeling now, I'd build my world over again even if I had to tear all of the old one down." Martin was now talking to himself, oblivious to his wife's presence, indifferent to her. "Happiness is waiting for me with her, with my little flower."

"Your Rose of Sharon?" Her tone was biting.

"If only I could say that! My Rose of Sharon!" It seemed to Mrs. Wade that the very room quivered with his low cry that was almost a groan. "I know what you're thinking," he went on, "but you know I have never loved you. You knew it when I married you, you must have." The twisting agony of it - that he could make capital out of the very crux of all her suffering. "I have never deceived you and I never intend to. My life with you hasn't been a Song of Solomon, but I'm not complaining."

"You're not complaining! I hope I won't start complaining, Martin."

"Well, now you know how I feel. I'll go on with the present arrangement between us, but I'm playing square with you - it's because there's no hope for me. If I thought she cared for me, I would go to her, right now, tonight, and pour out my heart to her, wife or no wife. Oh, Rose, have pity! It can't do you any harm if I drink a little joy - don't spoil her faith in me! Don't frighten her away. I can't bear the thought of her going out into the world to work. She's like a gentle little doe feeding on lilies - she doesn't dream of the pitfalls ahead of her. And she will never know - she doesn't even suspect how I feel towards her. She will meet some young fellow in town and marry. I'm too old for her - but Rose, you don't understand what it means to me to have her in the same house, to know that she is sleeping so near, so beautiful, so ready for love; that when I wake up tomorrow she will still be here."

Disarmed and partly appeased by the frankness of his confession, Mrs. Wade sat silently taking in each word, studying him with wet eyes, her lips almost blue, her breath a little short. The fire in his voice, the reality of his strange, terrible love, the eyes that gazed so sadly and so unexpectantly into space, the hands that seemed to have shed their weight of toil and clutched, too late, for the bright flowers of happiness - all filled her with compassion. Never had he looked so splendid. He seemed, in casting off his thongs, to have taken on some of the Herculean quality of his own magnificent gesture. It was as if their barnyard well had burst into a mighty, high-shooting geyser. To her dying day would she remember that surge of passion. To have met it with anger would have been of as little avail as the stamp of a protesting foot before the tremors of an earthquake.

She offered him the comforting directness which she might have given Bill. "I didn't know you felt so deeply, Martin. Life plays us all tricks; it's played many with me, and it's playing one of its meanest with you, for whatever happens you are going to suffer - far more than I am. You can believe it or not, but I'm sorry."

Martin felt oddly grateful to her; he had not expected this sense of understanding. She might have burst into wild tears. Instead, she was pitying him. More possessed of his usual immobility, he remarked:

"I must be a fool, a great, pathetic fool. I look into a girl's eyes and immediately see visions. I say a few words to her and she is kind enough to say a few to me and I see pictures of new happiness. I should have more sense. I don't know what is the matter with me."

Although countless answers leaped to his wife's tongue she made none but the cryptic: "Well, it's no use to discuss it any more tonight. We both need rest." But all the while that she was undressing with her usual sure, swift movements, and after she had finally slipped between the sheets, her mind was racing.

She was soon borne so completely out on the current of her own thoughts that she forgot Martin's actual presence. She remembered as if it were yesterday, the afternoon he came to the office and asked her to marry him. She wondered anew, as she had wondered a thousand times, if anything other than a wish for a housekeeper had prompted him. She remembered her misgivings - how she had read into him qualities which she had believed all these years were not there. But hadn't her intuition been justified, after all, by the very man she had seen tonight? Yes, her first feeling, that he was something finer, still in the rough, had been correct. She had thought it was his shyness, his unaccustomedness to women that had made him such a failure as a lover - and all the while it had been simply that she was not the right woman. When love touched him, he became a veritable white light.

All these years when he had been so cold, so hard toward her, it simply was because he disliked her. She remembered the day she was hurt, and the night her first baby came. Martin's brutality even now kindled in her a dull blazing anger, and as she realized what depths of feeling were in him, his callousness seemed intensified an hundred-fold. Well, she was having her revenge. All his life he had thwarted her, stolen from her, used her as one could not use even a hired hand, worked her more as a slave-driver hurries his underlings that profits may mount; now, by her mere existence, she was thwarting him. She saw him again as he had flashed before her when he had talked of Rose and she admitted bitterly to herself, what in her heart she had known all along - that if Martin could have loved her, she could have worshipped him. Instead, he had slowly smothered her, but she had at least a dignity in the community. He should not harm that. If they were unhappy, at least no one knew it. Her pride was her refuge. If that were violated she felt life would hold no sanctuary, that her soul would be stripped naked before the world.

But why was she afraid? Didn't Martin have his own position to think of? What if he had said nothing was to be compared to his new-found love for Rose. What stupidity on his part not to realize that it was his very position, power and money that commanded her respect. Did he command anything else from her? Mrs. Wade reviewed the evening. Yes, response had been in Rose's laugh, in every movement. Hadn't she always adored Martin, even as a tiny girl? Hadn't there always been some mystic bond between them? How she had envied them then. But if Martin were to go to her with only his love? From the depths of her observations of people she took comfort. He might stir his lovely Rose of Sharon to the uttermost, had he been free he might have won her for his wife - but would it be possible for fifty-four to hold the attention of twenty for long if he had nothing but his love to offer?

Such thoughts were hurrying through her heated mind as Martin slowly laid himself beside her. He said nothing, but lost himself in a flood of ceaseless ponderings. After stretching some of the tiredness out of his throbbing muscles, he relaxed and lay quietly, trying to recall exactly what he had said. Did his wife suspect that there might be no truth in the remark that Rose would never know how he felt toward her? At moments he felt that the girl already divined it, again he was not so sure. It was hard to be certain, but the more he thought about it the more hope he began to feel that she would yet be wholly his. Her admiration and trust belonged to him now, but there might be moral scruples which he would have to overcome. There would be the difficulty of convincing her that she would be doing her aunt no wrong. She would gain courage, however, from his own heedlessness. That same daring which he had just shown with the older Rose and which had impressed her into silence would eventually move his flower to him. He had thrown down the bars. Secrecy was now out of the question and it was well that he was moving thus in the open. Rose might shrink at first from the plain-spokenness of the situation, but this phase would soon pass and then the fact that she knew he was not hiding his love for her even from his wife would make it far easier to press his suit and possibly to bring it to a swift consummation.

He must win her! He must. He had been mad to admit to himself, much less to his Rag-weed, that there was any doubt of this outcome. It might take a few more days, a week, not longer than that. But what should he do when Rose gave the message to him? Could he go away with her? This bothered him for a while. Of course, he would have to. He could not send his wife away. The community would not tolerate this. Martin knew his neighbors. He did not care a snap for their good opinion, but he realized exactly how much they could hurt him if he violated their prejudices beyond a certain point. Fortunately, there are millions of communities in the world. This one would rise against him and denounce, another would accept them as pleasant strangers. He might be taken for Rose's father! He would fight this with tireless care. Yes, he would have to go away. But his business interests - what about his farm, his cattle, his machinery, his bank stock, his mortgages, his municipal bonds? How wonderful it would be if he could go with her to the station - his securities in a grip, his other possessions turned into a bank draft! But this woman lying at his side - the law gave her such a large share.

Cataclysmic changes were taking place in the soul of Martin Wade. The very thing which, without being able to name, he had dreaded a short week ago in the garage, was hovering over him, casting its foreboding shadow of material destruction. His whole system of values was being upset. He felt an actual revulsion against property. What was it all compared to his Rose? He would throw it at his wife's feet - his wife's feet and Bill's. Let them take every penny of it - no, not every penny. He would need a little - just a thousand or two to start with and then the rest would come easily, for he knew how to make money. And how liberal that would be.

He could see himself as he would go forth with Rose, leaving behind the woman he had never loved and all that he had toiled so many years to amass. It seemed fair - the property for which he had lusted so mercilessly left for the woman with whom he had lived so dully, left as the ransom to be paid for his liberty. So he and his Rose of Sharon would walk away - walk, because even the car would be surrendered - and he would be free with the only woman for whom he had ever yearned.

Would she be happy for long? His pride answered "yes," but against his will he pictured himself being dumped ruthlessly into the pitiless sixties while Rose still lingered in the glorious twenties. This was a most unpleasant reflection and Martin preferred to dismiss it. That belonged to tomorrow. He would wait until then to fight tomorrow's battles. His mind came back to the property again. Wasn't it rather impetuous to surrender all? Wouldn't it be unfair to Rose to be so generous to his wife? She had Bill. In a few years he would be old enough to run the farm. Until then, with his help and good hired hands, she could do it herself. Why not leave it and the goods on it to her and take the mortgages and bonds with him? Rose was joy. He could hold her more securely with comforts added to his great love. Her happiness had to be thought of, had to be protected.

He could tell that his wife was still awake. He might begin to talk and maybe they could arrange a settlement. But he was getting too tired for a discussion that might invite tears and even a fit of hysterics, like the one she had gone through before their first child came dead. He could see her still as she looked that morning in the barn crying: "You'll be punished for this some day - you will - you will. You don't love me, but some time you will love some one. Then you'll understand what it is to be treated like this - " It gave him the creeps now to remember it. It was like one of those old incantations; almost like a curse. What if some day his Rose should grow to be as indifferent, feel as little tenderness toward him as he had felt toward his wife at that moment. The pain of it made him break out into a fine sweat. But he hadn't understood. What had he understood until this love had come into his life! He would never do a thing as cruel as that now. Come to think of it, the older Rose wasn't acting like a bad sort. But then, when it came to a show-down she might not be so magnanimous as she had appeared tonight.

Mrs. Wade was still thinking. She also was measuring possibilities and clairvoyantly sensing what was going on in her husband's mind. She, too, was sure that Rose would capitulate to him. She felt a deep sympathy for the girl. Martin had said it himself - he was too old for her. Her happiness lay with youth. And yet, how could one be so certain? Love was so illusive, so capricious! Did it really bow to the accident of years? Had she, Rose Wade, the right to snatch from anyone's hands the most precious gift of life? Wouldn't she have sold her very soul, at one time, to have had Martin care for her like this? Oh, if the child were wise she would not hesitate! She would drink her cup of joy while it was held out to her brimming full. A strange conclusion for a staid churchwoman like Mrs. Wade, but her rich humanity transcended all her training. She wondered if there could be anything in the belief that there was waiting somewhere for each soul just one other. There were people, she knew, who thought that. Rose had drawn out all that was finest in Martin - she had transformed him into a lover, and if she wanted the man, himself, she could have him. But, decided his wife, he could not take with him the things which her sweat and blood had helped to create. She would give him a divorce, but her terms would be as brutal as the Martin with whom she had lived these twenty years, and who now took it for granted that she would let him do whatever he chose. She was to be made to step aside, was she, with no weapon with which to strike back and no armor with which to protect herself? Well, there was one way she might hit him - one. She would strike him in his weakest point - his belongings. Yes, Martin Wade might leave her but all his property must be left behind - every cent of it. There should be a contract to that effect; otherwise, she would fight as only a frenzied woman can fight.

The two of them, lying there side by side as quietly as if in death, each considered the issue settled. She would let him go without his property; Martin would leave with half of it. And through all the long wordless controversy, their little Rose of Sharon, a few yards away, slept as only a tired child can sleep.

VIII

THE DUST SMOTHERS

WHEN Martin opened his eyes, next morning, he realized with a start that he had overslept, which was a new experience for one whose life had been devoted so consistently to hard toil; and he saw with a sharper start, that his wife, who always got up about a half hour earlier than himself, was not even yet awake. He wondered what had come over him that he should have committed such a sin, and as his tired mind opened one of its doors and let the confused impressions flutter out, he countenanced a luxury as unusual as the impulse that had sent him townward the evening before to bring home the Victrola. Instead of jumping out hastily so that he might attend to his hungry, bellowing stock, he lay quietly marshalling the new incidents of his life into a parade which he ordered to march across the low ceiling.

He could not comprehend what the tornado had been about. There had been so little on which to base the excitement - so little that he was puzzled as to what had caused the scene with his wife. And as he reflected, it seemed highly unlikely to him that he would ever permit himself to do anything that might jeopardize his whole life, topple over the structure that decades of work had built. Why, it was scarcely less than suicidal to let a stranger come into his heart and maybe weaken his position. He remembered his last thought before falling asleep. It appeared unutterably rash, though when hit upon, it had been a decision that moderated a more extreme action. Now he realized that it was the very acme of foolishness deliberately to sacrifice half his fortune, especially the farm itself, to which he had given so many years of complete concentration. Certainly, if Rose were ready to be his, he might not hesitate even a second; but this flower was still to be won by him, and this morning, aware of what scant grounds he had upon which to venture any forecasts, he felt as full of doubt as he had been of confidence last night. It had been a saddening experience, but fortunate, for all that, inasmuch as nothing serious had come of it, except that he was greatly sobered. Martin could not understand that mysterious something which had risen up in his nature and threatened to wreck a carefully-built life. It was his first meeting with the little demon that rebels in a man after he thinks his character and his reactions thoroughly established, and he shuddered as he realized how close the strange imp had pulled him to the precipice. Yesterday, that precipice had seemed a new paradise; now it was a yawning chasm - and he drew back, frightened.

Cows, horses, sheep, pigs, chickens, turkeys, dogs, barn cats - all do not remain patient while the man who owns them lies in bed dreaming dreams. They wait a while and then get nervous. The many messages for food which they sent to Martin forced him to spring out of bed and hurry to them, for nothing is as unbearably insistent as a barn and yard full of living things clamoring their determination to have something to eat. As Martin ran to stop the bedlam, he saw the world as an enormous, empty stomach, at the opening of which he stood, hurling in the feed as fast as his muscles would permit. It was all there was to farming - raising crops and then shovelling the hay and the grain into these stomachs. Martin stood back a few feet and with loving eyes watched his animals enjoy their food. Here were the creatures he loved. The fine herd of Holstein cows - their big eyes looked at him with such trust! And their black and white markings - so spick and span with shininess because he threw salt on them that each cow might lick the other clean - their heavy milk veins, great udders, and backs as straight as a die - all appealed to his sense of the beautiful. "God Almighty!" he thought, "but they're wonders!

There's none like them west of Chicago." The mule colts, so huge and handsome, and oh, so knowing! made him chuckle his pride and satisfaction in a muttered: "Man's creation, are you, you fine young devils? Well, you're a credit, the lot of you, to whoever deserves it." His eyes wandered over the rest of his stock, swept his wide realm. It was all a very part of himself. Yes, here was his life - here was his world. It would be the height of folly to leave it.

At breakfast, his wife ate sullenly, refusing to be drawn into the conversation, but by a wise compression of her lips and a flicker of amusement in her eyes, which seemed to say: "Oh, if only you could see how absurd you appear," she contrived very cleverly to render Martin miserably self-conscious. Hampered by this new and unexpected feeling, his attempts to be pleasant fell flat and he lapsed into his old grimness, while Rose, eating quickly, confined her remarks to her determination to go to town in search of a job. Had Martin not talked as he had to his wife he would have been able, undoubtedly, to disregard her and to continue the line of chatter which he had hit upon so happily and which he had never suspected was in him. But the fact, not so much that she knew, but that from this vantage point of knowledge she was ridiculing him, was too much for even his self-possession. It made the light banter impossible. Especially, as there was no doubt that Rose did not seem anxious for it.

For Martin had not been the only member of that household who had held early communion with himself. The girl had sat long and dreamily at her dressing table - the dainty one of rich, dark mahogany that Uncle Martin's thoughtfulness had provided. It seemed unbelievable, but there was no use pretending she was mistaken - Uncle Martin, Aunt Rose's husband, was falling in love with her. She felt a little heady with the excitement of it. He was so different from the callow youths and dapper fellows who had heretofore worshipped at her shrine. There was something so imposing, so important about him. She was conscious that a man so much older might not appeal to many girls of her age, but it so happened that he did appeal to her. She would be able to have everything she wished, too - didn't she know how good, how kind, how tender he could be. And her heart yearned toward him - he was so clearly misunderstood, unhappy. But what about Aunt Rose? Well, then, why had she let herself get to be so ugly? She looked as if the greases of her own kitchen stove had cooked into her skin, thought the girl, mercilessly. Didn't she know there was such a thing as a powder puff? Women like that brought their own troubles upon themselves, that's what they did. And she was an old prude, too. Anyone could see with half an eye that she didn't like the idea of Uncle Martin learning to dance - why, she didn't even like his getting the Victrola - when it was just what both he and Bill had been wanting. But for all that she was her aunt, her own mother's sister and, poor dear, she was a good soul. It would probably upset her awfully and besides, oh well, it just wasn't right.

Before her mirror Rose blushed furiously, quite ashamed of the light way in which she had been leading Uncle Martin on. "But I haven't said one solitary thing auntie couldn't have heard," she justified herself. Oh, well, no harm had been done. But she mustn't stay here, that was certain. She wouldn't say so, or hurt their feelings, for she wanted to be on the best of terms with them always, but she would stop flirting with Uncle Martin and just turn him back into a dear good friend. She hoped she was clever enough to do that much. And the dark-brown curls received a brushing that left no doubt of the vigor of her decisions.

She insisted that she go to Fallon that morning.

"I've been here eight whole days, Uncle Martin," she announced firmly, "eight whole days and haven't tried to get a thing. It's terrible, isn't it, Aunt Rose, how lazy I am. I'm going to have Bill take me in right straight after breakfast."

"If you're so set on it, I'll see about your position this afternoon," conceded Martin reluctantly. "We'll drive in in the car."

"Oh, Uncle Martin," she coaxed innocently, "let me try my luck alone first. Bill can tell me who the different men are and if I know he's waiting for me outside in the buggy, it will keep me from being scared." And her young cousin, only too pleased with the proposed arrangement, chimed in with: "That's the stuff, Rose. Folks have got to go it on their own, to get anywhere."

By evening she had a position in an insurance agent's office with wages upon which she could live with fair decency. As it had rained all day and her employer wanted her to begin the next morning, she had the best possible excuse for renting a room in Fallon and asking Bill to ride in horseback with some things which she would ask Aunt Rose, over the telephone, to pack. It rained all the next day, too, and Sunday, when she met Mrs. Wade and Bill at church, she told them she had some extra typing she had promised to do by Monday. "No, auntie" this week it is really and truly just impossible, but next week - honest and true!" she insisted as the older woman seconded rather impersonally her son's urgent invitation to chicken and noodles.

Soon winter was upon them in good earnest, and Rose's visits "home," as she always called it, were naturally infrequent. By Christmas time, she was receiving attentions from Frank Mall, Nellie's second son, a young farmer of twenty-five.

To Mrs. Wade's everlasting credit, she never twitted Martin with this, although she knew it from Rose's own lips, a month before he heard of it through Bill. She was too grateful for their narrow escape to feel vindictive and might have convinced herself they had merely endured a bad nightmare if it had not been for the shiny Victrola; the sight of it underscored the whole experience and she wished there were some way to get rid of the thing, a wish that was echoed even more fervently by Martin. In the evenings they would sit around the cleared supper table, she doing odd jobs of mending, Martin reading, checking up the interest dates on his mortgages or making entries in his account book, while Bill at his books, would study to the accompaniment of record after record, blissfully unconscious of what a thorn in the flesh he and his music were to both his parents.

It was all so unpleasant. To Mrs. Wade it brought up pictures. And it made Martin feel sheepish - the way he had felt that afternoon, decades ago, as he sat in the bakery eating a chocolate ice-cream soda and watching her walk across the Square. He would have told Bill to quit playing it - more than once the sharp words were on his tongue - but memories of the enthusiasm he had evinced the night he brought it home kept him silent. He was afraid of what the boy might say, afraid he might put two and two together, so he let it stay, although with his usual caution he had arranged for a trial and would have felt justified in packing it back as soon as the roads had permitted. Illogically, he felt it was all Bill's fault that he must endure this annoyance.

That fall, the boy started to high school in Fallon, making the long daily ride to and from town on horseback. He was a good pupil and the hours he spent with his lessons were precious; they made the farm drift away. To his mind, which was opening like a bud, it seemed that history was the recorded romance of men who were everything but farmers. School books told fascinating stories of conquerors, soldiers, inventors, writers, engineers, kings, statesmen and orators. He would sit and dream of the doers of great deeds. When he read of Alexander the Great, Bill was he. He was Caesar and Napoleon, Washington and Lincoln, Grant and Edison and Shakespeare. When railroads were built in the pages of his American History, it was Bill, himself, no less, who was the presiding genius. His imagination constructed and levelled, and rebuilt and remade.

One beautiful November afternoon, in his Junior year, at the sound of the last bell, which usually found him cantering out of town, he went instead to the school reading-room, and, sitting down calmly, opened his book and slowly read. The clock ticked off the seconds he was stealing from his father;

counted the minutes that had never belonged to Bill before, but which now tasted like old wine on the palate. He cuddled down, lost to the world until five o'clock, when the building was closed. He left it only to march down a few blocks to the town's meager library, where another hour flew past. Gradually an empty feeling in his middle region became increasingly insistent, and briefly exploring his pockets, Bill decided upon a restaurant where he bought a stew and rolls for fifteen cents. Never had a supper tasted so satisfying. After it, he strolled around the town, feeling a pleasant warmth in his veins, a springiness to his legs, a new song in his heart. It was so good to be free to go where he pleased, to be his own master, if only for a stolen hour, to keep out of sight of a cow or a plow. He wondered why he had never done this before.

It was youth daring Fate, without show or bravado or fear; rolling the honey under his tongue and drawing in its sweetness; youth, that lives for the moment, that can be blind to the threatening future, that can forget the mean past; youth slipping along with some chewing-gum between his teeth and a warm sensation in his stew-crammed stomach, whistling, dreaming, happy; youth, that can, without premeditation, remain away from home and leave udders untapped and pigs unfed; sublime enigma; angering bit of irresponsibility to the Martins of a fiercely practical world. Bill was that rare kind of boy who could pull away from the traces just when he seemed most thoroughly broken to the harness.

It was ten o'clock before he got his pony out of the livery barn and started for home. Even on the way, he refused to imagine what would happen. He entered the house quietly, as though to tell his father that it was his next move, and setting his bundle of books on a chair, he glanced at his mother. She was at the stove, where an armful of kindling had been set off to take the chill out of the house. She looked at him mysteriously, as though he were a ghost of some lost one who had strayed in from a graveyard, but she said nothing. Bill did not even nod to her. He fumbled with his books, as though to keep them from slipping to the floor when, quite obviously, they were not even inclined to leave the chair. Rose let her eyes fall and then slide, under half-closed lids, until they had Martin in her view. She looked at him appealingly, but he was staring at a paper which he was not reading. He had been in this chair for two hours, without a word, pretending to be studying printed words which his mind refused to register. Martin had done Bill's share of the chores, with unbelief in his heart. He had never imagined such a thing. Who would have thought it could happen - a son of his!

His wife broke the silence with:

"What happened, Billy? Were you sick?"

"No, mother, I wasn't sick."

Martin was still looking at his paper, which his fists gripped tightly.

"Then you just couldn't get home sooner, could you? Something you couldn't help kept you away, didn't it?"

Bill shook his head slowly. "No," he answered easily. "I could have come home much sooner."

"Billy, dear, what DID happen?" She was beginning to feel panicky; he was courting distress.

"Nothing, mother. I just felt like staying in the reading-room and reading - "

"Oh, you HAD to do some lessons, didn't you! Miss Roberts should have known better - "

"I didn't have to stay in - I wanted to."

Martin still kept silent, his eyes looking over the newspaper wide open, staring, the muscles of his jaw relaxed. The boy was quick to sense that he was winning - the simple, non-resistance of the lamb was confounding his father.

"I wanted to stay. I read a book, and then I took a walk, and then I dropped in at the restaurant for a bite, and then I walked around some more, and then I went to a movie."

"Billy, what are you saying?"

Martin, slowly putting down his paper, remarked without stressing a syllable:

"You had better go to bed, Bill; at once, without arguing."

Bill moved towards the parlor, as though to obey. At the door he stopped a moment and said: "I wasn't arguing; I was just answering mother. She wanted to know."

"She does not want to know."

"Then I wanted her to know that I don't intend to work after school any more. I'll do my chores in the morning, but that's all. From now on nobody can MAKE me do anything."

"I am not asking you to do anything but go to bed."

"I don't intend to come home tomorrow afternoon until I'm ready. Or any afternoon. And if you don't like it - "

"Billy!" his mother cried; "Billy! go to bed!"

The boy obeyed.

Bill was fifteen when this took place. The impossible had happened. He had challenged the master and had won. Even after he had turned in, his father remained silent, feeling a secret respect for him; mysteriously he had grown suddenly to manhood. Martin was too mental to let anger express itself in violence and, besides, strangely enough, he felt no desire to punish; there was still the dislike he had always felt for him -

his son who was the son of this woman, but though he would never have confessed aloud the satisfaction it gave him, he began to see there was in the boy more than a little of himself.

"Poor Billy," his mother apologized; "he's tired."

"He didn't say he was tired - "

"Then he did say he was tired of working evenings."

"That's different."

"Yes, it's different, Martin; but can you make him work?"

"No, I don't intend to try. He isn't my slave."

With overwhelming pride in her eyes, pride that shook her voice, she exclaimed: "Not anybody's slave, and not afraid to declare it. Billy is a different kind of a boy. He doesn't like the farm - he hates it - "

"I know."

"He loathes everything about it. Only the other day he told me he wished he could take it and tear it board from board, and leave it just a piece of bleak prairie, as it was when your father brought you here, Martin."

"You actually mean he said he would tear down what took so many years of work to build? This farm that gives him a home and clothes and feeds him?"

"He did, Martin. And he meant it - there was hatred burning in his eyes. There's that in his heart which can tear and rend; and there's that which can build. Oh, my unhappy Billy, my boy!"

"Don't get hysterical. What do you want me to do? Have I said he must work?"

"No, but you have tried to rub it into his soul and it just can't be done. You're not to be blamed for being what you are, nor is Billy - I'll milk his cows."

"I'm not asking that."

"But I will, Martin."

"And let him stand by and watch you?"

"Put it that way if you will. Billy must get away from here. I see that now."

"I haven't suggested it."

"But I do. I want him to be happy. We'll let him board in Fallon the rest of the year. The butter and egg money will be enough to carry him through. It won't cost much. If we don't send him, he'll run away. I know him. He's my boy, and your son, Martin. I won't see him suffer in a strange world, learning his lessons from bitter experiences. I want him to be taken care of."

"Very well, have it as you say. I'm not putting anything in the way. I thought this was his home, but I see it isn't. It isn't a prison. He can go, and good luck go with him." And after a long silence: "He would tear down this farm - the best in the county! Tear it down - board from board!"

IX

MARTIN'S SON SHAKES OFF THE DUST

THE very next day, Mrs. Wade rented a room for Bill in the same home in which Rose boarded, and for the rest of the winter she and Martin went on as before - working as hard as ever and making money even faster, while peace settled over their household, a peace so profound that, in her more intuitive moments, Bill's mother felt in it an ominous quality.

The storm broke with the summer vacation and the boy's point-blank refusal to return to farm work. His father laid down an ultimatum: until he came home he should not have a cent even from his mother, and home he should not come, at all, until he was willing to carry his share of the farm work willingly, and without further argument. "You see," he pointed out to his wife, "that's the thanks I get for managing along without him this winter. The ungrateful young rascal! If he doesn't come to his senses shortly - "

"Oh, Martin, don't do anything rash," implored Mrs. Wade. "Nearly all boys go through this period. Just be patient with him."

But even she was shaken when his Aunt Nellie, over ostensibly for an afternoon of sociable carpet-rag sewing, began abruptly: "Do you know what Bill is doing, Rose?"

"Working in the mines," returned his mother easily. "Isn't it strange, Nellie, that he should be digging coal right under this farm, the very coal that gave Martin his start?"

"Well, I'm not going to beat about the bush," continued her sister-in-law abruptly. "He's working in the mines all right, but he isn't digging coal at all, though that would be bad enough. I wouldn't say a word about it, but I think you ought to know the truth and put a stop to such a risky business - he's firing shots."

Rose's heart jumped, but she continued to wind up her large ball with the same uninterrupted motion.

"Are you sure?"

"I made Frank find out for certain. It's an extra dangerous mine because gas forms in it unusually often, and he gets fifteen dollars a day for the one hour he works. There's a contract, but he's told them he's twenty-one, and when you prove he's under age they'll make him stop."

Rose still wound and wound, her clear eyes, looking over her glasses, fixed on Nellie.

"It's bad enough, I'll say," rapped out the spare, angular woman, "to have everybody talking about the way Martin has ditched his son, without having the boy scattered to bits, or burned to a cinder. Already he's been blown twenty feet by one windy shot, and more than once he's had to lie flat while those horrible gases burned themselves out right over his head. His 'buddie,' the Italian who fires in the other part of the mine at the same time, told Harry Brown, the nightman, and he told Frank, himself. Why, they say if he'd have moved the least bit it would have fanned the fire downward and he'd have been in a fine mess. Sooner or later all shot-firers meet a tragic end. You want to put your foot down, Rose, and put it down hard - for once in your life - if you can," she added, half under her breath.

"It isn't altogether Martin's fault," began Rose, but Nellie cut her off with a short: "Now, don't you tell me a word about that precious brother of mine! It's as plain to me as the nose on your face that between his bull-headed hardness and your wishy-washy softness you're fixing to ruin one of the best boys God ever put on this earth."

"I'll talk to Billy," Rose promised.

It was the first time she ever had found herself definitely in opposition to her boy, but she felt serene in the confidence of her own power to dissuade him from anything so perilous. She understood the general routine of mining, and had been daily picturing him going down in the cage to the bottom, traveling through a long entry until he was under his home farm and located in one of the low, three-foot rooms where a Kansas miner must stoop all day. Oh, how it had hurt - that thought of those fine young shoulders bending, bending! She had visualized him filling his car, and mentally had followed his coal as it was carried up to the surface to be dumped into the hopper, weighed and dropped down the chute into the flat cars. Of course, there was always the danger of a loosened rock falling on him, but wasn't there always the possibility of accidents on a farm, too? Didn't the company's man always go down, first, into the mine to test the air and make certain it was all right? Rose had convinced herself that the risk was not so great, after all, though she could not help sharing a little of her husband's wonder that the boy could prefer to work underground instead of in the sweet, fresh sunshine. But she had thought it was because in the desperation of his complete revolt from Martin's domination anything else seemed to him preferable. Now, in a lightning flash, she understood. This reaction from a life whose duties had begun before sun-up and ended long after sundown, made danger seem as nothing in comparison with the marvellous chance to earn a comfortable living with only one hour's work a day.

Her conversation with Bill proved that she had been only too right. The boy was intoxicated with his own liberty. "I know I ought to have told you, mother," he confessed. "I wanted to. Honest, I did, but I was afraid you'd worry, though you needn't. The man who taught me how to fire has been doing it over twenty years. A lot of it's up to a fellow, himself. You can pretty near tell if the air is all right by the way it blows - the less the better it is. And if you're right careful to see that the tool-boxes the boys leave are all locked - so's no powder can catch, you know - and always start lighting against the air, so that if there's gas and it catches the fire'll blow away from you instead of following you up - and if you examine the fuses to see they're long enough and the powder is tamped in just right - each miner does that before he leaves and lots of firers just give 'em a hasty once-over instead of a real look - and then shake your heels good and fast after you do fire - "

"Billy!" Rose was white. "I can't bear it - to hear you go on so lightly, when it's your life, your LIFE, you're playing with. For my sake, son, give it up."

With an odd sinking of the heart, she observed the expression in his face which she had seen so often in his father's - the one that said as plainly as words that nothing could shake his determination. "A fellow's got a right to some good times in this world," he said very low, "and I'm getting mine now. I'm not going to grind away and grind away all my life like father and you've done. If anything did happen I'd have had a chance to dream and think and read instead of getting to be old without ever having any fun out of it all. Maybe you won't believe it, but some days for hours I just lie in the sun like a darky boy, not even thinking. Gee! it feels great! And sometimes I read all day until I have to go to the mine. There's one thing I'm going to tell you square," he went on, a firm ring in his voice, boyish for all its deep, bass note, "I'm never going back to the farm, never! Mother," he cried, suddenly, coming over to take her hand in both his. "Will you leave father? We could rent a little house and you'd have hardly anything to do. I'm making more than lots of men with families. And I'd give you my envelope without opening it every pay-day." "Oh, Billy, you don't know what you're saying! I couldn't leave your father. I couldn't think of it."

"What I don't see is how you can stand it to stay with him. He's always been a brute to you. He's never cared a red cent for either of us."

Rose was abashed before the harsh logic of youth. "Oh, son," she murmured brokenly, "there are things one can't explain. I suppose it may seem strange to you - but his life has been so empty. He has missed so much! Everything, Billy."

"Then it's his own fault," judged the boy. "If ever anybody's always had his own way and done just as he darn pleased it's father. I wish he'd die, that's what I wish."

"Bill!" His mother's tone was stern.

"There you are!" he marvelled. "You must have wished it lots of times yourself. I know you have. Yet you always talk as if you loved him."

In Rose's eyes, the habitual look of patience and understanding deepened. How could Bill, as yet scarcely tried by life, comprehend the purging flames through which she had passed or realize time's power to reveal unsuspected truths.

"When you've been married to a man nearly twenty-two years and have built up a place together, there's bound to be a bond between you," she eluded. "He just lives for this farm. It's almost as dear to him as you are to me, son, and it's a wonderful heritage, Bill, a magnificent heritage. Just think! Two generations have labored to build it out of the dust. Your father's whole life is in it. Your father's and mine. And your grandmother's. If only you could ever come to care for it!"

Bill fidgeted uneasily. "You mean you want me to go on with it?" he demanded. "You want me to come back to it, settle down to be a farmer - like father?"

The tone in which he asked this question made Rose choose her words carefully.

"What are your plans, son? What do you want to be - not just now, but finally?"

"I can't see what difference it makes what a fellow is – except that in one business a man makes more than in another. And I can't see either that it does a person a bit of good to have money. I'm having more fun right now than father or you ever had - more fun than anybody I know. Mother," and his face was solemn as if with a great discovery, "I've figured it out that it's silly to do as most people - just live to work. I'm going to work just enough to live comfortably. Not one scrap more, either. You can't think how I hate the very thought of it."

Rose sighed. Couldn't she, indeed! She understood only too well how deeply this rebellion was rooted. The hours when he had been dragged up from the far shores of a dreamful slumber to shiver forth in the chill darkness to milk and chore, still rankled. Those tangy frosty afternoons, when he had been forced to clean barns and plow while the other boys went rabbit and possum hunting or nutting, were afternoons whose loss he still mourned. Nothing had yet atoned for the evenings when he had been torn from his reading and sent sternly to bed because he must get up so early. Always work had stolen from him these treasures - dreams, recreation and knowledge. He had been obliged to fight the farm and his father for even a modicum of them - the things that made life worth living. And the irony of it - that eventually it would be this farm and Martin's driving methods which, if he became reconciled to his father, would make it possible for him to drink all the fullness of leisure.

It was too tragic that the very thing which should have stood for opportunity to the boy had been used to embitter him and drive him into danger. But he must not lose his birthright. An almost passionate desire welled in Rose's heart to hold on to it for him. True, she too had been a slave to the farm. Yet not so much a slave to it, she distinguished, as to Martin's absorption in its development. And of late years there had been for her, running through all the humdrum days, a satisfaction in perfecting it. In her mind now floated clearly the ideal toward which her husband was striving. She had not guessed how much it had become her own until she felt herself being drawn relentlessly by Bill's quiet, but implacable determination to have her leave it all behind. If only he would try again, she felt sure all would be so different! His father had learned a lesson, of that she was positive, and though he would not promise it, would not be so hard on the boy. And with this new independence of Bill's to strengthen her, they could resist Martin more successfully as different issues came up. She could manage to help her boy get what he wanted out of life without his having to pay such a terrible price as, the mine on one hand, and his father's displeasure on the other, might exact, for she knew that if he persisted too long, the break with Martin could never be bridged and that in the end his father would evoke the full powers of the law to disinherit him and tie her own hands as completely as possible in that direction.

But she was far too wise to press such arguments in her son's present mood. They would have to drift for a while, she saw that clearly, until she could gradually impress upon him how different farming would be if he were his own master. In time, he might even come to understand how much Martin needed her.

"Say you will," Bill, pleading, insistent, broke in on her train of reflections, "I've always dreamed of this day, when we'd go away, and now it's come. I can take care of you."

As he stood there, a glorious figure in his youthful self-confidence, a turn of his head reminded her a second time of Martin, recalling sharply the way her husband had looked the night he told her of his love for the other Rose. He had been bothered by no fine qualms about abandoning herself. She thought of his final surrender of love to wisdom. It was only youth that dared pursue happiness - to purchase delicious idleness by gambling with death. Billy was her boy. His dreams and hopes should be hers; her way of life, the one that gave him the most joy. She would follow him, if need be, to the end of the earth.

"Very well, son," she said simply, her voice breaking over the few words. "If a year from now you still feel like this, I'll do as you wish."

"You don't know how I hate him," muttered the boy. "It's only when I'm tramping in the woods, or in the middle of some book I like that I can forgive him for living. No, mother, I don't mean all that," he laughed, giving her a bear-like hug.

It was in this more reasonable side, this ability to change his point of view quickly when he became convinced he was wrong, that Mrs. Wade now put her faith. She would give him plenty of rope, she decided, not try to drive him. It would all come right, if she only waited, and she prayed, nightly, with an increasing tranquillity, that he might be kept safe from harm, taking deep comfort in the new light of contentment that was gradually stealing into his face. After all, each one had to work out his destiny in his own way, she supposed.

It was less than a month later that her telephone rang, and Rose, calmly laying aside her sewing and getting up rather stiffly because of her rheumatism, answered, thinking it probably a call from Martin, who had left earlier in the evening, to wind up a little matter of a chattel on some growing wheat. It had just begun to rain and she feared he might be stuck in the road somewhere, calling to tell her to come for him. But it was not Martin's voice that answered.

"Mrs. Wade?"

"Yes."

"Why" - there was a forbidding break that made her shudder. A second later she convinced herself that it seemed a natural halt - people do such things without any apparent cause; but she could not help shaking a little.

"Is it about Mr. Wade?" and as she asked this question she wondered why she had spoken her husband's name when it was Bill's that really had rushed through her mind.

"No, ma'am, it ain't about Martin Wade I'm callin' you up, it ain't him at all - "

"I see." She said this calmly and quietly, as though to impress her informant and reassure him. "What is it?" It was almost unnecessary to ask, for she knew already what had happened, knew that the boy had flung his dice and lost.

"It's your son, Mrs. Wade; it's him I'm a-callin' about. We're about to bring him home to you - an' - and I thought it'd be better to call you up first so's you might expect us an' not take on with the suddenness of it all. This is Brown - Harry Brown - the nightman at the mine down here. We've got the ambulance here and we're about ready to start." There was an evenness about the strange voice that she understood better than its words. If Bill had been hurt the man would have been quick and jerky in his speaking as though he were feeling the boy's pain with him; but he was so even about it all - as even as Death.

"Then I'll phone for Dr. Bradley so he'll be here by the time you come," said Rose, wondering how she could think of so practical a thing. Her mind had wrapped itself in a protecting armor, forbidding the shock of it all to strike with a single blow. She couldn't understand why she was not screaming.

"You can - if you want to, but Bill don't need him, Mrs. Wade, - he's dead."

Slowly she hung up the receiver, the wall still around her brain, holding it tight and keeping her nerves taut, afraid to release them for fear they might snap. She stood there looking at the receiver as her hands came together.

As though she were talking to a person instead of the telephone before her, she gasped: "So - so THIS is what it has all been for - this. Into the world, into Martin's world - and this way out of it. Burned to death - Billy."

The rain had lessened a little and now the wind began to shake the house, rattle the windows and scream as it tore its way over the plains. The sky flared white and the world lighted up suddenly, as though the sun had been turned on from an electric switch. At the same instant she saw a bolt of lightning strike a young tree by the roadside, heard the sharp click as it hit and then watched the flash dance about, now on the road, now along the barbed wire fencing. Then the world went black again. And a rumble quickly grew to an earth-shaking blast of thunder. It was as though that tree were Billy - struck by a gush of flying fire. The next bolt broke above the house, and the light it threw showed her the stripling split and lying on the ground. In the impenetrable darkness she realized that the house fuse of their Delco system must have been blown out, and she groped blindly for a match. She could hear the rain coming down again, now in rivers. There was unchained wrath in the downpour, viciousness. It was a madman rushing in to rend and tear. It frothed, and writhed, and spat hatred. Rose shook as though gripped by a strong hand. She was afraid - of the rain, the lightning, the thunder, the darkness; alone there, waiting for them to bring her Billy. She was too terrified to add her weeping to the wail of the wind - it would have been too ghastly. Would she never find a match! As she lit the lamp, like the stab of a needle in the midst of agony, came the thought of how long it had been after Martin had put in his electrical system and connected up his barns before she had been permitted to have this convenience in the house. What would he think now? She wished he were home. Anyone would be better than this awful waiting alone. She could only stand there, away from the window, looking out at the sheets of water running down the panes and shivering with the frightfulness and savageness of it all.

Her ears caught a rumble, fainter than thunder, and the splash of horses' hoofs - "it's too muddy for the motor ambulance," she thought, mechanically. "They're using the old one," and her heart contracting, twisting, a queer dryness in her throat, she opened the door as they stopped, her hand shading the lamp against the sudden inrush of wind and rain. "In there, through the parlor," she said dully, indicating the new room and thinking, bitterly, as she followed them, that now, when it could mean nothing to Billy, Martin would offer no objections to its being given over to him.

The scuffling of feet, the low, matter-of-fact orders of a directing voice: "Easy now, boys - all together, lift. Watch out; pull that sheet back up over him," and a brawny, work-stooped man saying to her awkwardly: "I wouldn't look at him if I was you, Mrs. Wade, till the undertaker fixes him up," and she was once more alone.

As if transfixed, she continued to stand, looking beyond the lamp, beyond the bed on which her son's large figure was outlined by the sheet, beyond the front door which faced her, beyond - into the night, looking for Martin, waiting for him to come home to his boy. She asked herself again and again how she had been so restrained when her Billy had been carried in. After what seemed interminable ages, she heard heavy steps on the back porch and knew that her husband had returned at last. He brought in with him a gust of wind that caused the lamp to smoke. She held it with both hands, afraid that she might drop it, and carrying it to the dining-room table set it down slowly, looking at him. He seemed huger than ever with his hulk sinking into the gray darkness behind him. There was something elephantine about him as he stood there, soaked to the skin, bending forward a little, breathing slowly and deeply, his fine nostrils distending with perfect regularity, his face in the dim light, yellow, with the large lines almost black. He was hatless and his tawny-gray hair was flat with wetness, coming down almost to his eyes, so clear and far-seeing.

"What's the matter with the lights? Fuse blown out?" he asked, spitting imaginary rain out of his mouth.

Rose did not answer.

"Awful night for visiting," Martin announced roughly, as he took off his coat. "But it was lucky I went, or all would have been pretty bad for me. Do you know, that rascal was delivering the wheat to the elevator - wheat on which I held a chattel - and I got to Tom Mayer just as he was figuring up the weights. You should have seen Johnson's face when I came in. He knew I had him cornered. 'Here,' I said, 'what's up?' And that lying rascal turned as white as death and said something about getting ready to bring me a check. I told him I was much obliged, but I would take it along with me - and I did. Here it is - fourteen hundred dollars, plus interest. And I got it by the skin of my teeth. I didn't stop to argue with him for I saw the storm coming on. I went racing, but a half mile north I skidded into the ditch. I really feel like leaving the car there all night, but it would do a lot of damage. I'll have to get a team and drag it in. I call it a good day's work. What do you say?" He looked at her closely, for the first time noticing her drawn face and far-away look.

"What's the matter? You look goopy - "

Rose settled herself heavily in the rocker close to the table.

"You're not sick, are you?"

She shook her head a few times and answered: "He's in there - "

"Who?" Martin straightened up ready for anything.

"Billy - "

"Oh!" A light flashed into Martin's face. "So he has come back, has he? Back home? What made him change toward this place? Is he here to stay?"

"No, Martin - "

"Then if he hasn't come to his senses, what is he doing here - here in my house, the home he hates - "

"He doesn't hate it now," Rose replied, struggling for words that she might express herself and end this cruel conversation, but all she could do was to point nervously toward the spare room.

"What is he doing in there? It's the one spot that Rose can call her own, poor child."

"He's on the bed, Martin - "

"What's the matter with the davenport he's always slept on? Is he sick? What in heaven's name is going on in this house?"

As Martin started toward the bedroom, his wife opened her lips to tell him the truth but the words refused to come; at the same instant it struck her that not to speak was brutal, yet just. She would let Martin go to this bed with words of anger on his lips, with feelings of unkindness in his heart. She would do this. Savage? Yes, but why not? There seemed to be something fair about it. Then her heart-strings pulled more strongly than ever. No; it was too hard. She must stop him, tell him, prepare him. But before the words came, he was out of the room and when she spoke he did not hear her because of the rain.

He saw the vague lines of the boy's body, hidden by the sheet, and thought quickly, "Bill's old ostrich-like trick," and while at the same instant something told him that a terrible thing had happened, the idea did not register completely until he had his hand on the linen. Then, with a short yank, he pulled away the cover and saw the boy's head. Dark as it was, it was enough to show him the truth. With a quick move he covered him again. There was a smeary wetness on his fingers, which he wiped away on the side of his trousers. They were drenched with rain, but he distinguished the sticky feel of blood leaving his hand as he rubbed it nervously.

His first emotion was one of anger with Rose. He was sure she had played this sinister jest deliberately to torture him and he had fallen into the trap. He wanted to rush back into the other room and strike her down. He would show her! But he dismissed this impulse, for he did not want her to see him like this, no hold on himself and his mind without direction. Sitting there, she would have the advantage. Without so much as a sound except for the slight noise he made in walking, Martin went through the parlor towards the front door and out to the steps, where he leaned for a moment against the weather-boarding, letting the rain fall on him as he stared dully down at the ground. It felt good to stand there. No eyes were on him, and the rain was refreshing. This had been too much for him. Never had he known himself to be so near to bewilderment. How fortunate that he had escaped by this simple trick of leaving the house. Then he thought of the car - a half-mile north - and the horses in the stable. He must do something. He would bring the car into the garage. It was relieving to hurry across the dripping grass toward the barn. How wonderful it was to keep the body doing something when the breath in him was short, his heart battering like an engine with burned-out bearings, his brain in insane chaos. As he applied a match to the lantern he thought of his wife again, and his face regained its scowl.

Only when he had his great heavy team in the yard, his lantern hanging from his arm, the reins in his hands, and was pulling back with all his strength as he followed the horses - only then did he permit himself to think about the tragedy that had befallen.

"He's dead - killed," he groaned. "It had to come. Shot-firers don't last long. Whoa, there, Lottie; not so fast, Jet, whoa!" His protesting team in control again, he trudged heavily behind. "It's terrible to die that way - not a chance in a thousand. And a kid of sixteen didn't have the judgment - couldn't have. But Bill knew what he was facing every evening.

He didn't go in blindly. They'll blame me, as though it was my fault. I didn't want him to go there. I wanted him to take a hand here, to run the place by himself in good time. It was his mother who sent him away first." He went on like that, justifying himself more positively as excuse after excuse suggested itself.

Not until he had convinced himself that he was in no way responsible, did he allow his heart to beat a little for this boy of his. "Poor Bill," he thought on, "it has been a tough game for him. Lost in the shuffle. Born into something he didn't like and trying to escape, only to get caught. What did he expect out of life, anyway? Why didn't he learn that it's only a lot of senseless pain? Every moment of it pain - from coming into the world to going out. Oh, Bill, why didn't you learn what I know? You had brains, boy, but it would have been better if you had never used them. I've brains, too, but I've always managed to keep them tied down - buckled to the farm, to investments, and work - thinking about things that make us forget life. It's all dust and dust, with rain once in a while, only the rain steams off and it's dust again."

Martin began to review the course of his own past, and smiled bitterly. Others were able to live the same kind of an existence, but, unlike himself, took it as a preparation for another day, another existence which, it seemed to him, was measured and cut to order by professionals who understood how to fix up the meaning of life so that it would soothe and satisfy. He thought how much better it was to be a dumb, unquestioning beast, or a human being conscious of his soul, than to be as he was - alone, a materialist, who saw the meaninglessness of matter and whose mind, in some manner which he did not understand, had developed a slant that made him doubt what others accepted so easily as facts. Martin knew he was bound to things of substance but he followed the lure of property and accumulation as he might have followed some other game had he learned it, knowing all along that it was a delusion and at the same time acknowledging that for him there was nothing else as sufficing.

How simple, if Bill's future could be a settled thing in his mind as it was to the boy's mother. Or his own future! If only he could believe - then how different it would be for him. He could go on placidly and die with a smile. But he could not believe. His atheism was both mental and instinctive. It was something he could not understand, and which he knew he could never change, try as he might. Take this very evening. Here was death in his home. And he was escaping a lot of anguish, not by praying for Bill's soul or his own forgiveness, but by the simple process of harnessing a team and dragging a car through the mud. It was a great game, work was - the one weapon with which to meet life. This was not a cut and dried philosophy with him, but a glimmer that, though always suggesting itself but dimly, never failed when put to the test. Martin felt better. He began to probe a little farther, albeit with an aimlessness about his questions that almost frightened him. He asked himself whether he loved Bill, now that he was dead, and he had to admit that he did not. The boy had always been something other than he had expected - a disappointment. Did he love anyone? No. Not a person; not even any longer that lovely Rose of Sharon who had flowered in his dust for a brief hour. His wife? God Almighty, no. Then who? Himself? No, his very selfishness had other springs than that. He was one of those men, not so uncommon either, he surmised, who loved no one on the whole wide earth.

When he re-entered the house, he found his wife still seated in the rocker, softly weeping, the tears flowing down her cheeks and dropping unheeded into her lap. He pitied her.

"I feel as though he didn't die tonight," she mourned, looking at Martin through full eyes. "He died when he was born, like the first one."

"I know how you feel," said Martin, sympathy in his voice.

"I made him so many promises before he came, but I wasn't able to keep a single one of them."

"I'm sorry; I wish I could help you in some way."

"Oh, Martin, I know you're not a praying man - but if you could only learn."

Martin looked at her respectfully but with profound curiosity.

"There must be an answer to all this," Rose went on brokenly. "There must! Billy is lying in the arms of Jesus now - no pain, only sweet rest. I believe that."

"I'm glad you have the faith that can put such meaning into it all."

"Martin, I want to pray for strength to bear it."

"Yes, Rose."

"You'll pray with me, won't you?"

"You just said I wasn't a praying man."

"Yes, but I can't pray alone, with him in there alone, too, and you here with me, scoffing."

"I can't be other than I am, Rose; but you pray, and as you pray I'll bow my head."

X

INTO THE DUST-BIN

WITH the loss of her boy, time ceased to exist for Rose. The days came and went, lengthening into years, full of duties, leaving her as they found her, outwardly little changed and habitually calm and kind, but inwardly sunk in apathy. She moved as if in a dream, seeming to live in a strange world that would never again seem real - this world without Billy. Occasionally, she would forget and think he was out in the field or down in the mine; more rarely still, she would slip even further backward and wonder what he was about in his play. During these moments she would feel normal, but some object catching her eye would jerk her back to the present and the cruel truth. She and Martin had less than ever to say to each other, though in his own grim way he was more thoughtful, giving her to understand that there were no longer any restrictions laid upon her purchasing, and even suggesting that they remodel the house; as if, she thought impassively, at this late day, it could matter what she bought or in what she lived. His one interest in making money, just as if they had some one to leave it to, puzzled her. Always investing, then reinvesting the interest, and spending comparatively little of his income, his fortune had now reached the point where it was growing rapidly of its own momentum and, as there was nothing to which he looked forward, nothing he particularly wanted to do, he set himself the task of making it cross the half million mark, much as a man plays solitaire, to occupy his mind, betting against himself, to give point to his efforts.

Yet, it gave him a most disconcerting, uncanny start, when one bright winter day, he faced the fact that he, too, was about to be shovelled into the great dust-bin. Death was actually at his side, his long, bony finger on his shoulder and whispering impersonally, "You're next." "Very much," thought Martin, "like a barber on a busy Saturday." How odd that here was something that had never entered into his schemes, his carefully worked out plans! It seemed so unfair - why, he had been feeling so well, his business had been going on so profitably, there was something so substantial to the jog of his life, there seemed to be something of the eternal about it. He had taken ten-year mortgages but a few days ago, and had bought two thousand dollars' worth of twenty-year Oklahoma municipals when he could have taken an earlier issue which he had rejected as maturing too soon. He had forgotten that there was a stranger who comes but once, and now that he was here, Martin felt that a mean trick had been played on him. He cogitated on the journey he was to take, and it made him not afraid, but angry. It was a shabby deal - that's what it was - when he was so healthy and contented, only sixty-one and ready to go on for decades - two or three at least - forced, instead, to prepare to lay himself in a padded box and be hurriedly packed away. It had always seemed so vague, this business of dying, and now it was so personal - he, Martin Wade, himself, not somebody else, would suffer a little while longer and then grow still forever.

He would never know how sure a breeder was his new bull - the son of that fine creature he had imported; two cows he had spotted as not paying their board could go on for months eating good alfalfa and bran before a new herdsman might become convinced of their unreadiness to turn the expensive feed into white gold; he had not written down the dates when the sows were to farrow, and they might have litters some-where around the strawstack and crush half the little pigs. His one hundred and seventy-five acres of wheat had had north and south dead furrows, but he had learned that this was a mistake in probably half the acreage, where they should be east and west. It would make a great difference in the drainage, but a new plowman might think this finickiness and just go ahead and plow all of it north and south, or all of it east and west and this would result in a lower yield - some parts of the field would get soggy and the wheat might get a rust, and other parts drain too readily, letting the ground become parched and break into cakes, all of which might be prevented. And there was all that manure, maker of big crops. He knew only too well how other farmers let it pile up in the barnyard to be robbed by the sun of probably twenty per cent of its strength. He figured quickly how it would hurt the crops that he had made traditional on Wade land. He considered these things, and they worried him, made him realize what a serious thing was death, far more serious than the average person let himself believe.

Martin had gone to the barn a week before to help a cow which was aborting. It had enraged him when he thought what an alarming thing this was - abortion among HIS cows - in Martin Wade's beautiful herd! "God Almighty!" he had exclaimed, deciding as he took the calf from the mother to begin doctoring her at once. He would fight this disease before it could establish a hold. Locking the cow's head in an iron stanchion, he had shed his coat, rolled up his right sleeve almost to the shoulder, washed his hand and arm in a solution of carbolic and hot water, carefully examining them to make sure there was no abrasion of any kind. But despite his caution, a tiny cut so small that it had escaped his searching, had come in contact with the infected mucous membrane and blood poisoning had set in. And here he was, lying in bed, given up by Doctor Bradley and the younger men the older physician had called into consultation and who had tried in vain to stem the spread of poison through his system. Martin was going to die, and no power could save him. The irony of it! This farm to which he had devoted his life was taking it from him by a member of its herd.

Martin made a wry little grimace of amusement as he realized suddenly that even at the very gate of death it was still on life, his life, that his thoughts dwelt. In these last moments, it was the tedious, but stimulating, battle of existence that really occupied his full attention. He would cling to it until the last snap of the thin string. This cavern of oblivion that was awaiting him, that he must enter - it was black and now more than ever his deep, simple irreligion refused to let fairy tales pacify him with the belief that beyond it was everlasting daylight. Scepticism was not only in his conscious thought but in the very tissues of his mind.

He remembered how his own father had died on this farm - he had had no possessions to think about; only his loved ones, his wife and his children; but he had brought them here that they might amass property out of Martin's sweat and the dust of the prairie. Now he, the son, dying, had in his mind no thought of people, but of this land and of stock and of things. And how strangely his mind was reacting to it. His concern was not who should own them all, but what would actually be the fate of each individual property child of his. Why, he had not even written a will. It would all go to his wife, of course, and how little he cared to whom she left it. He would have liked, perhaps, to have given Rose Mall twenty-five thousand or so - so she could always be independent of that young husband of hers - snap her fingers at him if he got to driving her too hard, and crushing out the flower-like quality of her - but his wife wouldn't have understood, and he had hurt her enough, in all conscience. The one thing he might have enjoyed doing, he couldn't. Outside of that he didn't care who got it. She could leave it to whomever she liked when her turn came. Not to whom it went, but what would happen to it - that was what concerned him.

By his side, Rose, sitting so motionless that he was scarcely conscious of her presence, was dying with him. With that peculiar gift of profoundly sympathetic natures she was thinking and feeling much of what he was experiencing. It seemed to her heart-breaking that Martin must be forced to abandon the only things for which he cared. He had even sacrificed his lovely Rose of Sharon for them - she had never been in any doubt as to the reason for that sudden emotional retreat of his seven years before. And she knew his one thought now must be for their successful administration.

He had worked so hard always and yet had had so little happiness, so little real brightness out of life. She felt, generously, with a clutching ache, that with all the disappointments she had suffered through him - from his first broken promises about the house to his lack of understanding of their boy which had resulted in Billy's death - with even that, she had salvaged so much more out of living than he. A great compassion swelled within her; all the black moments, all the long, gray hours of their years together, seemed suddenly insignificant. She saw him again as he had been the day he had proposed marriage to her and for the first time she was sure that she could interpret the puzzling look that had come into his eyes when she had asked him why he thought she could make him happy. What had he understood about happiness? With a noiseless sob, she remembered that he had answered her in terms of the only thing he had understood - work. And she saw him again, too, as he had been the night he had so bluntly told her of his passion for Rose. It seemed to her now, free of all rancor, unutterably tragic that the only person Martin had loved should have come into his life too late.

He was not to be blamed because he had never been able to care for herself. He should never have asked her to marry him - and yet, they had not been such bad partners. It would have been so easy for her to love him. She had loved him until he had killed her boy; since then, all her old affection had withered. But if it really had done so why was she so racked now? She felt, desperately, that she could not let him go until he had had some real joy. To think that she used to plan, cold-bloodedly, when Billy was little, all she would do if only Martin should happen to die! The memory of it smote her as with a blow. She looked down at the powerful hand lying so passively, almost, she would have said, contentedly, in her own. How she had yearned for the comfort of it when her children were born. She wondered if Martin realized her touch, if it helped a little. If it had annoyed him, he would have said so. It came to her oddly that in all the twenty-seven years she and her husband had been married this was the very first time he had let her be tender to him. Oh, his life had been bleak. Bleak! And she with such tenderness in her heart. It hadn't been right. From the depths of her rebellion and forgiveness, slow tears rose. Feeling too intensely, too mentally, to be conscious of them she sat unmoving as they rolled one by one down her cheeks and dropped unheeded.

"Rose," he called with a soft hoarseness, "I want to talk to you."

"Yes, Martin," and she gave his fingers a slight squeeze as though to convince him that she was there at his side. He felt relieved. It was good to feel her hand and be sure that if his body were to give its final sign that life had slipped away someone would be there to know the very second it had happened. It was a satisfactory way to die; it took a little of the loneliness away from the experience.

"Rose," he repeated. It sounded so new, the yearning tone in which he said it - "Rose!" It hurt. "Isn't it funny, Rose, to go like this - not sick, no accident - just dying without any real reason except that I absorbed the poison through a cut so small my eyes couldn't see it."

"It's a mystery, dear," the little word limped out awkwardly, "but God's ways are not ours."

"Not a mystery," he corrected, "just a heap of tricks; funny ones, sad ones, sensible ones, and crazy ones - and of all the crazy ones this is the worst. But, what's the use? If there's a God, as you believe, it doesn't do any good to argue with Him, and if it's as I think and there's no God, there's no one to argue with. But never mind about that now - it's no matter. You'll listen carefully, won't you, Rose?"

"Yes, Martin."

"This abortion in the herd. You know what a terrible thing it is."

"I certainly do; it's the cause of your leaving me."

"Rose, I know you'll be busy during the next few days - me dying, the things that have to be arranged, the funeral and all that. But when it's all over, you'll let that be the first thing, won't you?"

"Yes, the very first thing, if you wish it."

"I do. Get Dr. Hurton on the job at once, and have him fight it. He knows his business. Let him come twice a day until he's sure it's out of the herd. Keep that new bull out of the pasture. And if Hurton can't clean it up, you'd better get rid of the herd before it gets known around the country. You know how news of that kind travels. Don't try to handle the sale yourself. If you do, it'll be a mistake. The prices will be low if you get only a county crowd."

"Neighbors usually bid low," she agreed.

"Run up to Topeka and see Baker - he's the sales manager of the Holstein Breeders' Association. Let him take charge of it all - he's a straight fellow. He'll charge you enough - fifteen per cent of the gross receipts, but then he'll see to it that the people who want good stuff will be there. He knows how and where to advertise. He's got a big list of names, and can send out letters to the people that count. He'll bring buyers from Iowa down to Texas. Remember his name - Baker."

"Yes, Martin - Baker."

"I think you ought to sell the herd anyway," he went on. "I know you, Rose; you'll be careless about the papers - no woman ever realizes how important it is to have the facts for the certificates of registry and transfer just right. I'm afraid you'll fall down there and get the records mixed. You won't get the dates exact and the name and number of each dam and sire. Women are all alike there - they never seem to realize that a purebred without papers is just a good grade."

Rose made no comment, while Martin changed his position slowly and lost himself in thought.

"Yes, I guess it's the only thing to do - to get rid of the purebred stuff. God Almighty! It's taken me long enough to build up that herd, but a few weeks from now they'll be scattered to the four winds. Well, it can't be helped. Try to sell them to men who understand something of their value. And that reminds me, Rose. You always speak of them as thoroughbreds. It always did get on my nerves. That's right for horses, but try to remember that cows are purebreds. You'll make that mistake before men who know. Those little things are important. Remember it, won't you?"

"Thoroughbred for a horse, and purebred for a cow," Rose repeated willingly.

"When you get your money for the stock put it into mortgages - first mortgages, not seconds. Let that be a principle with you. Many a holder of a second mortgage has been left to hold the sack. You must remember that the first mortgage comes in for the first claim after taxes, and if the foreclosure doesn't bring enough to satisfy more than that, the second mortgage is sleeping on its rights."

"First mortgages, not seconds," said Rose.

"And while I'm on that, let me warn you about Alex Tracy, four miles north and a half mile east, on the west side of the road. He's a slippery cuss and you'll have to watch him."

"Alex Tracy, four miles north - "

"You'll find my mortgage for thirty-seven hundred in my box at the bank. He's two coupons behind in his interest. I made him give me a chattel on his growing corn. Watch him - he's treacherous. He may think he can sneak around because you're a woman and stall you. He's just likely to turn his hogs into that corn. Your chattel is for growing corn, not for corn in a hog's belly. If he tries any dirty business get the sheriff after him."

"It's on the GROWING corn," said Rose.

"And here's another important point - taxes. Don't pay any taxes on mortgages. What's the use of giving the politicians more money to waste? Hold on to your bank stock and arrange to have all mortgages in the name of the bank, not in your own. They pay taxes on their capital and surplus, not on their loans. But be sure to get a written acknowledgment on each mortgage from Osborne. He's square, but you can't ever tell what changes might take place and then there might be some question about mortgages in the bank's name."

"Keep them in the bank's name," said Rose.

"And a written acknowledgment," Martin stressed.

"A written acknowledgment," she echoed.

For probably fifteen minutes he lay without further talk; then, a little more weariness in his voice than she had ever known before, he began to speak again.

"I've been thinking a great deal, Rose." There was still that new tenderness in the manner in which he pronounced her name, that new tone she had never heard before and which caused her to feel a little nervous. "I've been thinking, Rose, about the years we've lived together here on a Kansas prairie farm - "

"It lacks just a few months of being twenty-eight years," she added.

"Yes, it sounds like a long time when you put it that way, but it doesn't seem any longer than a short sigh to me lying here. I've been thinking, Rose, how you've always got it over to me that you loved me or could love me - "

"I've always loved you, Martin - deeply."

"Yes, that's what's always made me so hard with you. It would have been far better for you if you hadn't cared for me at all. I've never loved anybody, not even my own mother, nor Bill, nor myself for that matter." Their eyes shifted away from each other quickly as both thought of one other whom he did not mention. "I wasn't made that way, Rose. Now you could love anything - lots of women are like that, and men, too. But I wasn't. Life to me has always been a strange world that I never got over thinking about and trying to understand, and at the same time hustling to get through with every day of it as fast as I could by keeping at the only thing I knew which would make it all more bearable. There's a lot of pain in work, but it's only of the muscles and my pain has always been in the things I've thought about. The awful waste and futility of it all! Take this farm - I came here when this was hardly more than a desert. You ought to have seen how thick the dust was the first day we got down here. And I've built up this place. You've helped me. Bill didn't care for it - even if he had lived, he'd never have stayed here. But you do, in spite of all that's happened."

"Yes, Martin, I do," she returned fervently. "It's a wonderful monument to leave behind you - this farm is."

His eyes grew somber. "That's what I've always thought it would be," he answered, very low. "I've felt as if I was building something that would last. Even the barns - they're ready to stand for generations. But this minute, when the end is sitting at the foot of this bed, I seem to see it all crumbling before me. You won't stay here. Why should you - even if you do for a few years you'll have to leave it sometime, and there's nothing that goes to rack and ruin as quickly as a farm - even one like this."

"Oh, Martin, don't think such thoughts," she begged. "Your fever is coming up; I can see it."

"What has it all been about, that's what I want to know," he went on with quiet cynicism. "What have I been sweating about - nothing. What is anyone's life? No more than mine. We're all like a lot of hens in a backyard, scratching so many hours a day. Some scratch a little deeper than those who aren't so skilled or so strong. And when I stand off a little, it's all alike. The end is as blind and senseless as the beginning on this farm - drought and dust."

Martin closed his eyes wearily and gave a deep sigh. To his wife's quickened ears, it was charged with lingering regret for frustrated plans and palpitant with his consciousness of life's evanescence and of the futility of his own success.

She waited patiently for him to continue his instructions, but the opiates had begun to take effect and Martin lapsed into sleep. Although he lived until the next morning, he never again regained full consciousness.

XI

THE DUST SETTLES

ROSE'S grief was a surprise to herself; there was no blinking the fact that her life was going to be far more disrupted by Martin's death than it had been by Bill's. There were other differences. Where that loss had struck her numb, this quickened every sensibility, drove her into action; more than that, as she realized how much less there was to regret in the boy's life than in his father's, how much more he had got out of his few short years, the edge of the older, more precious sorrow, dulled. During quite long periods she would be so absorbed in her thoughts of Martin that Bill would not enter her mind. Was it possible, that this husband who with his own lips had confessed he had never loved her, had been a more integral part of herself than the son who had adored her? What was this bond that had roots deeper than love? Was it merely because they had grown so used to each other that she felt as if half of her had been torn away and buried, leaving her crippled and helpless? Probably it would have been different if Bill had been living. Was it because when he had died, she still had had Martin, demanding, vital, to goad her on and give the semblance of a point to her life, and now she was left alone, adrift? She pondered over these questions, broodingly.

"I suppose you'll want to sell out, Rose," Nellie's husband, Bert Mall, big and cordial as Peter had been before him, suggested a day or two after the funeral. "I'll try to get you a buyer, or would you rather rent?"

"I haven't any plans yet, Bert," Mrs. Wade had evaded adroitly, "it's all happened so quickly. I have plenty of time and there are lots of things to be seen to." There had been that in her voice which had forbidden discussion, and it was a tone to which she was forced to have recourse more than once during the following days when it seemed to her that all her friends were in a conspiracy to persuade her to a hasty, ill-advised upheaval.

Nothing, she resolved, should push her from this farm or into final decisions until a year had passed. She must have something to which she could cling if it were nothing more than a familiar routine. Without that to sustain and support her, she felt she could never meet the responsibilities which had suddenly descended, with such a terrific impact, upon her shoulders.

In an inexplicable way, these new burdens, her black dress - the first silk one since the winter before Billy came - and the softening folds of her veil, all invested her with a new and touching majesty that seemed to set her a little apart from her neighbors.

Nellie had been frankly scandalized at the idea of mourning. "Nobody does that out here - exceptin' during the services," she had said sharply to her daughter-in-law when Rose had told her of the hasty trip she and her aunt had made to the largest town in the county. "Folks'll think it's funny and kind o' silly. You oughtn't to have encouraged it."

"Oh, Mother Mall, I didn't especially," the younger woman had protested. "She just said in that quiet, settled way she has, that she was going to - she thought it would be easier for her. And I believe it will, too," she added, feeling how pathetic it was that Aunt Rose had never looked half so well during Uncle Martin's life as she had since his death.

"Oh, well," Mall commented, "Rose always was sort of sentimental, but there's not many like her. She's right to take her time, too. It'll be six or eight months, anyway, before she can get things lined up. She's got a longer head than a body'd think for. Look at the way she run that newspaper office when old Conroy died."

"That was nearly thirty years ago," commented his wife crisply, "and Rose's got so used to being bossed around by Martin that she'll find it ain't so easy to go ahead on her own."

With her usual shrewdness, Nellie had surmised the chief difficulty, but it dwindled in real importance because of the fact that Rose so frequently had the feeling that Martin merely had gone on a journey and would come home some day, expecting an exact accounting of her stewardship. His instructions were to her living instructions which must be carried out to the letter.

She had attended with conscientious promptness to checking the trouble that had brought about his death. "I promised Mr. Wade it should be the first thing," she had explained to Dr. Hurton. 'You'll let it be the first thing, won't you?' Those were his very words. He depended on us, Doctor."

When the time came to plan definitely for the disposal of the purebred herd, she went herself to Topeka to arrange details with Baker. She was constantly thinking: "Now, what would Martin say to this?" or "Would he approve of that?" And her conclusions were reached accordingly. The sale itself was an event that was discussed in Fallon County for years afterwards. The hotel was crowded with out-of-town buyers. Enthused by the music from two bands, even the local people bid high, and through it all, Rose, vigilant, remembered everything Martin would have wanted remembered. She felt that even he would have been satisfied with the manner in which the whole transaction was handled, and with the financial results.

She began to take a new pleasure in everything, the nervous pleasure one takes when going through an experience for what may be the last time. The threshing - how often she had toiled and sweated over those three days of dinners and suppers for twenty-two men. Now she recalled, with an aching tightness about her heart, how delicious had been her relaxation, when, the dinner dishes washed, the table reset and the kitchen in scrupulous order with the last fly vanquished, she and Nellie had luxuriated in that exquisite sense of leisure that only women know who have passed triumphantly through a heavy morning's work and have everything ready for the evening. Later there had been the stroll down to the field in the shade of the waning afternoon, to find out what time the men would be in for supper; and the sheer delight of breathing in the pungent smell of the straw as it came flying from the funnel, looking, with the sinking sun shining through it, like a million bees swarming from a hive, while the red-brown grain gushed, a lush stream, into the waiting wagon.

"It always makes me think of a ship sailing into port, Nellie," Rose had once exclaimed, "the crop coming in. It gives me a queer kind of giddiness, makes me feel like laughing and crying all at once," to which her sister-in-law had returned with more than her usual responsiveness: "Yes, it's the most excitin' time of the year, unless it's Christmas."

More nebulous were the memories of those early mornings when she had paused in the midst of getting breakfast to sniff in the clover-laden air and think how wonderful it would be if only she needn't stay in the hot, stuffy kitchen but could be free to call Bill and go picnicking or loaf deliciously under one of the big elms. Most precious of all - the evenings she and her boy had sat in the yard, with the cool south breeze blowing up from the pasture, the cows looking on placidly, the frogs fluting rhythmically in the pond, the birds chirping their good-night calls, and the dip and swell of the farm land pulling at them like a haunting tune, almost too lovely to be endured. Oh, there had been moments all the sweeter and more poignant because they had been so fleeting.

As she passed successfully through one whole round of planting, harvesting and garnering of grain, she began to realize her own ability and to be tempted more and more seriously to remain on the farm. She understood it, and Martin would have liked her to run it. If it had not been for the problem of keeping dependable hired hands and the sight of the mine-tipple, which, towering on the adjoining farm, reminded her more and more constantly of Bill, she would not even have considered the offer of Gordon Hamilton, one of Fallon's leading business men, to buy her whole section.

"There's a bunch going into this deal, together, Rose," Bert Mall explained. "They want to run a new branch of their street car line straight through here and they're going to plat this quarter into streets and lots. The rest they'll split up into several farms and rent for the present. It's a speculation, of course, but the way the mines are moving north and west it's likely this'll be a thickly settled camp in another two or three years."

"But they only offer seventy-five an acre," Rose expostulated, "and it's worth more than that as farm land. There's none around here as fertile as Martin made this - and then, all the improvements!"

"They'll have to dispose of them second-hand. It's a pity they're in exactly the wrong spot. Well, of course, I'm not advising you, Rose," he added, "but forty-five thousand ain't to be sneezed at, is it, when it comes in a lump and you own only the surface? You may wait a long while before you get another such bid. Seems to me you've worked hard enough. I'd think you'd want a rest."

In the end, Mrs. Wade capitulated to what, as Martin had foreseen so clearly, was sooner or later inevitable. She was a little stunned by the vast amount of available money now in her possession and at her disposal. "But it's all dust in my hands," she thought sadly. "What do I want of so much? It's going to be a terrible worry. I don't even know who to leave it to," and she sighed deeply, pressing her hands, with her old, characteristic gesture, to her heart. Everybody would approve, she supposed, if she left it to Rose and Frank - her niece and Martin's nephew - but she couldn't quite bring herself to welcome that idea - not yet. And anyway it might be better to divide it among more people, so that it would bring more happiness.

Her own needs were simple. The modest five-room house which she purchased was set on a pleasant paved street in Fallon and was obviously ample for her. She hoped that during part of each year she could rent the extra bed-room to some one, preferably a boy, like Bill, who was attending high school. There was a barn for her horse and the one cow she would keep, a neat little chicken-house for the twenty-five hens that would more than supply her with eggs and summer fries, and a small garage for Martin's car. It would seem very strange, she thought, to have so few things to care for and she wondered how she would fill her time, she whose one problem always had been how to achieve snatches of leisure. She saw herself jogging on and on, gradually getting to be less able on her feet, a little more helpless, until she was one of those feeble old ladies who seem at the very antipodes of the busy mothers they have been in their prime. How could it be that she who had always been in such demand, so needed, so driven by real duties, should have become suddenly such a supernumerary, so footloose, and unattached?

But when it came to that, wasn't Fallon full of others in the same circumstances? It was not an uncommon lot. There was Mrs. McMurray. Rose remembered over what a jolly household she had reigned before she, too, had lost her husband and three children instead of just one, like Billy. Two of them had been grown and married. Now she was living in a little cottage, all alone, doing sewing and nursing, yet always so brave and cheerful; not only that, but interested, really interested in living. And Mrs. Nelson. Her children were living and married and happy, but she had given up her home, sold it - the pretty place with the hospitable yard that used to seem to be fairly spilling over with wholesome, boisterous boys and chatty, beribboned little girls. She was rooming with a family, taking her meals at a restaurant, keeping up her zest in tomorrow by running a shop. She thought of how her friend, Mrs. Robinson, gracious, democratic woman of wide sympathies that she was, had lived alone after David Robinson's death, taking his place as president of the bank, during the years her only daughter, Janet, had been off at college and later travelling around the country "on the stage" - of all things for a daughter of Fallon. When hadn't the town been full of these widowed, elderly women made childless alike by life and by death? What others had met successfully, she could also, she told herself sternly, and still the old Rose, still struggling toward happiness, she tried to think with a little enthusiasm of her new life, of the things she would do for others. One recreation she would be able to enjoy to her heart's content when she moved into town - the movies. They would tide her over, she felt gratefully. When she was too lonely, she would go to them and shed her own troubles and problems by absorption in those of others. She who had been married for years and had borne two children without ever having had the joy of one overwhelming kiss, would find romance at last, for an hour, as she identified herself with the charming heroines of the films.

She was to surrender the farm and the crops as they stood in June, but as there was to be no new immediate tenant in her old house it was easily arranged that she could continue in it until the cottage in Fallon would be empty in September.

Meanwhile, preparations were begun for the new car line which would pass where the big dairy barn was standing. As the latter went down, board by board, it seemed to Mrs. Wade that this structure which, in the building, had been the sign and symbol of her surrender and heartbreak, now in its destruction, typified Martin's life. It was as if Martin, himself, were being torn limb from limb. All that he had built would soon be dust. The sound of the cement breaking under the heavy sledges, was almost more than she could bear. It was a relief to have the smaller buildings dragged bodily to other parts of the farm.

Only once before in her memory had there been such a summer and such a drought. The corn leaves burned to a crisp brown, the ground cracked and broke into cakes and dust piled high in thick, velvety folds on weeds and grass. It seemed too strange for words to see others harvest the wheat and to know that the usual crop could not be put in.

Rose was thankful when her last evening came. Most of her furniture had been moved in the morning, her boxes had left in the afternoon, and the last little accessories were now piled in the car. As, hand on the wheel, she paused a moment before starting, she was conscious of a choking sensation. It was over, finished - she, the last of Martin, was leaving it, for good. Before her rolled the quarter section, except for the little box-house, as bare of fences and buildings as when the Wades had first camped on it in their prairie schooner. With what strange prophetic vision had Martin foreseen so clearly that all the construction of his life would crumble. Would Jacob and Sarah Wade have had the courage to make all their sacrifices, she wondered, if they had known that she and she alone, daughter of a Patrick and Norah Conroy, whom they had never seen, would some day stand there profiting by it all? She thought of the mortgages in the bank and the bonds, of the easier life she seemed to be entering. How strange that she whom Grandfather and Grandmother Wade had not even known, she whom Martin had never loved, should be the one to reap the real benefits from their planning, and that the farm itself, for which her husband had been willing to sacrifice Billy and herself, should be utterly destroyed. A sudden breeze caught up some of the dust and whirling it around let it fall. "Martin's life," thought Rose, "it was like a handful of dust thrown into God's face and blown back again by the wind to the ground."

Choose from Thousands of 1stWorldLibrary Classics By

A. M. Barnard
Ada Leverson
Adolphus William Ward
Aesop
Agatha Christie
Alexander Aaronsohn
Alexander Kielland
Alexandre Dumas
Alfred Gatty
Alfred Ollivant
Alice Duer Miller
Alice Turner Curtis
Alice Dunbar
Ambrose Bierce
Amelia E. Barr
Amory H. Bradford
Andrew Lang
Andrew McFarland Davis
Andy Adams
Anna Sewell
Annie Besant
Annie Hamilton Donnell
Annie Payson Call
Annonaymous
Anton Chekhov
Arnold Bennett
Arthur Conan Doyle
Arthur M. Winfield
Arthur Ransome
Atticus
B.H. Baden-Powell
B. M. Bower
Baroness Emmuska Orczy
Baroness Orczy
Basil King
Bayard Taylor
Ben Macomber
Bertha Muzzy Bower
Bjornstjerne Bjornson
Booth Tarkington
Boyd Cable
Bram Stoker
C. Collodi
C. E. Orr
C. M. Ingleby
Carolyn Wells
Catherine Parr Traill
Charles A. Eastman
Charles Dickens

Charles Dudley Warner
Charles Farrar Browne
Charles Ives
Charles Kingsley
Charles Klein
Charles Amory Beach
Charles Hanson Towne
Charles Lathrop Pack
Charles Whibley
Charles Willing Beale
Charlotte M. Braeme
Charlotte M. Yonge
Charlotte Perkins Stetson
Clair W. Hayes
Clarence Day Jr.
Clarence E. Mulford
Clemence Housman
Confucius
Cornelis DeWitt Wilcox
Cyril Burleigh
D. H. Lawrence
Daniel Defoe
David Garnett
Dinah Craik
Don Carlos Janes
Donald Keyhoe
Dorothy Kilner
Dougan Clark
Douglas Fairbanks
E. Nesbit
E.P.Roe
E. Phillips Oppenheim
Earl Barnes
Edgar Rice Burroughs
Edith Van Dyne
Edith Wharton
Edward J. O'Biren
Edward S. Ellis
Edwin L. Arnold
Eleanor Atkins
Eliot Gregory
Elizabeth Gaskell
Elizabeth McCracken
Elizabeth Von Arnim
Ellem Key
Emerson Hough
Emilie F. Carlen
Emily Dickinson
Enid Bagnold

Enilor Macartney Lane
Erasmus W. Jones
Ernie Howard Pie
Ethel Turner
Ethel Watts Mumford
Eugenie Foa
Eugene Wood
Eustace Hale Ball
Evelyn Everett-green
Everard Cotes
F. H. Cheley
F. J. Cross
Federick Austin Ogg
Ferdinand Ossendowski
Francis Bacon
Francis Darwin
Frances Hodgson Burnett
Frances Parkinson Keyes
Frank Gee Patchin
Frank Harris
Frank Jewett Mather
Frank L. Packard
Frank V. Webster
Frederic Stewart Isham
Frederick Trevor Hill
Frederick Winslow Taylor
Friedrich Kerst
Friedrich Nietzsche
Fyodor Dostoyevsky
G.A. Henty
G.K. Chesterton
Gabrielle E. Jackson
Garrett P. Serviss
Gaston Leroux
George A. Warren
George Ade
Geroge Bernard Shaw
George Durston
George Ebers
George Eliot
George Gissing
George MacDonald
George Meredith
George Orwell
George Sylvester Viereck
George Tucker
George W. Cable
George Wharton James
Gertrude Atherton

Grace E. King
Grace Gallatin
Grant Allen
Guillermo A. Sherwell
Gulielma Zollinger
Gustav Flaubert
H. A. Cody
H. B. Irving
H.C. Bailey
H. G. Wells
H. H. Munro
H. Irving Hancock
H. Rider Haggard
H. W. C. Davis
Hamilton Wright Mabie
Hans Christian Andersen
Harold Avery
Harold McGrath
Harriet Beecher Stowe
Harry Houidini
Helent Hunt Jackson
Helen Nicolay
Hendrik Conscience
Hendy David Thoreau
Henri Barbusse
Henrik Ibsen
Henry Adams
Henry Ford
Henry Frost
Henry James
Henry Jones Ford
Henry Seton Merriman
Henry W Longfellow
Herbert A. Giles
Herbert N. Casson
Herman Hesse
Homer
Honore De Balzac
Horace Walpole
Horatio Alger Jr.
Howard Pyle
Howard R. Garis
Hugh Lofting
Hugh Walpole
Humphry Ward
Ian Maclaren
Inez Haynes Gillmore
Irving Bacheller
Israel Abrahams
Ivan Turgenev
J.G.Austin

J. Henri Fabre
J. M. Barrie
J. Macdonald Oxley
J. S. Fletcher
J. S. Knowles
J. Storer Clouston
Jack London
Jacob Abbott
James Allen
James Andrews
James Baldwin
James DeMille
James Joyce
James Lane Allen
James Lane Allen
James Oliver Curwood
James Oppenheim
James Otis
James R. Driscoll
Jane Austen
Janet Aldridge
Jens Peter Jacobsen
Jerome K. Jerome
John Burroughs
John Cournos
John F. Kennedy
John Gay
John Glasworthy
John Habberton
John Joy Bell
John Kendrick Bangs
John Milton
John Philip Sousa
Jonas Lauritz Idemil Lie
Jonathan Swift
Joseph A. Altsheler
Joseph Carey
Joseph Conrad
Joseph E. Badger Jr
Joseph Hergesheimer
Joseph Jacobs
Jules Vernes
Julian Hawthrone
Julie A Lippmann
Justin Huntly McCarthy
Kakuzo Okakura
Kenneth Grahame
Kenneth McGaffey
Kate Langley Bosher
Kate Langley Bosher
Katherine Cecil Thurston

Katherine Stokes
L. A. Abbot
L. T. Meade
L. Frank Baum
Latta Griswold
Laura Lee Hope
Laurence Housman
Lawrence Beasley
Leo Tolstoy
Leonid Andreyev
Lewis Carroll
Lewis Sperry Chafer
Lilian Bell
Lloyd Osbourne
Louis Hughes
Louis Tracy
Louisa May Alcott
Lucy Fitch Perkins
Lucy Maud Montgomery
Lydia Miller Middleton
Lyndon Orr
M. Corvus
M. H. Adams
Margaret E. Sangster
Margaret Vandercook
Margret Penrose
Maria Edgeworth
Maria Thompson Daviess
Mariano Azuela
Marion Polk Angellotti
Mark Overton
Mark Twain
Mary Austin
Mary Catherine Crowley
Mary Cole
Mary Hastings Bradley
Mary Roberts Rinehart
Mary Rowlandson
M. Wollstonecraft Shelley
Maud Lindsay
Max Beerbohm
Myra Kelly
Nathaniel Hawthrone
Nicolo Machiavelli
O. F. Walton
Oscar Wilde
Owen Johnson
P.G. Wodehouse
Paul and Mabel Thorne
Paul G. Tomlinson
Paul Severing

Percy Brebner
Peter B. Kyne
Plato
R. Derby Holmes
R. L. Stevenson
R. S. Ball
Rabindranath Tagore
Rahul Alvares
Ralph Bonehill
Ralph Henry Barbour
Ralph Victor
Ralph Waldo Emmerson
Rene Descartes
Rex Beach
Rex E. Beach
Richard Harding Davis
Richard Jefferies
Richard Le Gallienne
Robert Barr
Robert Frost
Robert Gordon Anderson
Robert L. Drake
Robert Lansing
Robert Lynd
Robert Michael Ballantyne
Robert W. Chambers
Rosa Nouchette Carey
Rudyard Kipling
Samuel B. Allison

Samuel Hopkins Adams
Sarah Bernhardt
Sarah C. Hallowell
Selma Lagerlof
Sherwood Anderson
Sigmund Freud
Standish O'Grady
Stanley Weyman
Stella Benson
Stephen Crane
Stewart Edward White
Stijn Streuvels
Swami Abhedananda
Swami Parmananda
T. S. Ackland
T. S. Arthur
The Princess Der Ling
Thomas A. Janvier
Thomas A Kempis
Thomas Anderton
Thomas Bailey Aldrich
Thomas Bulfinch
Thomas De Quincey
Thomas H. Huxley
Thomas Hardy
Thomas More
Thornton W. Burgess
U. S. Grant
Valentine Williams

Various Authors
Vaughan Kester
Victor Appleton
Virginia Woolf
Walter Camp
Walter Scott
Washington Irving
Wilbur Lawton
Wilkie Collins
Willa Cather
Willard F. Baker
William Dean Howells
William le Queux
W. Makepeace Thackeray
William W. Walter
Winston Churchill
Yei Theodora Ozaki
Yogi Ramacharaka
Young E. Allison
Zane Grey